GHOST LOVE

GHOSTLOVE

DENNIS MAHONEY

PUBLISHING

New York, NY

Printed in the United States of America
10 9 8 7 6 5 4 3 2 1

Ig Publishing
Box 2547
New York, NY 10163

www.igpub.com

ISBN: 978-1-632461-05-6 (paperback)

To Coley, Jack, and Bones

1. MY HAUNTED MOTHER

"Every room we enter is immediately haunted," my mother once said.

She was a librarian with an effervescent love of the occult, but I never knew if she truly believed in otherworldly forces prior to the winter of 1998, when she entered a mysterious brownstone and only part of her came back out.

Her name was Charlotte. She had auburn hair, starburst freckles on her shoulders and cheeks, and a captivating gangliness that reminded me more of my second-grade classmates than any of their mothers. She laughed whenever she sneezed. She hugged a lot. She daydreamed in a wonderstruck, concentrated way that made me want to know whatever she was thinking.

Her favorite library patron was a man named Leonard Stick. He was remarkably active at the age of ninety, and he credited his vigor to meaningful work and a lifelong diet of root vegetables. Mr. Stick shared my mother's love of the occult and was, according to her, a man of direct experience.

She delighted in helping him locate obscure texts through interlibrary loan. They were peculiar books on ultraspecific subjects: children's teeth, winding shrouds, the effects of gravity on ethereal bodies. Many of the books existed as single copies in remote libraries, and although my mother always succeeded in filling his requests, the books would often vanish from the Dewey Decimal System, and sometimes even from my mother's memory, as soon as he returned them.

In early January of '98, Mr. Stick abruptly stopped visiting the library. My mother grew concerned and visited his brownstone, where she discovered he was ill and couldn't leave the house. From that day on, she visited Mr. Stick every day after work, and often on the weekends, and sometimes late at night. I'd grown up watching my mother knitting hats for charity drives, holding hands with lost children, and wafting hornets out of the house instead of whacking them with magazines, and so her devotion to a lonely old man was unsurprising.

I was seven that year, the only child of a happy marriage, and thought of death as a fascinating misfortune other people suffered. Over dinner one night, I asked my parents if Mr. Stick was dying.

"Of course," my father said. "He's ninety years old. Unless he has a lightning rod that animates bodies. Has he got one of those?"

"Nope," my mother said.

"Odds are grim, then. He ought to be in a nursing home," he added, not unkindly.

"He only needs some company," my mother said.

My father raised his fork, pretending to be stern. "Don't get into his will. We'll end up with a house full of shrunken heads and potions. And don't let him haunt you."

"What if I like being haunted?" she asked.

My father turned to me and said, "When I was your age, I learned that when a person very special to us dies, they float around in heaven, watching us forever. I think of that now whenever I'm on the toilet."

"Not to worry," my mother said. "Even ghosts get afraid."

I liked the way my parents talked. There seemed to be a

signal underneath their words, a secret language they alone understood.

"Only you can haunt me. No one else," my father said.

My mother sipped her wine. "I'll haunt you both. I promise."

Most nights, my mother put me to bed and told me about her visits to Mr. Stick's house. She said that his brownstone was special—that either its brick and iron were conducive to supernatural forces, or the space itself had something of an otherworldly porousness. The building was a ghostly double-image of itself, like a picture painted brightly over an older, stranger picture. The house's deepest secrets were subliminal. Infused. It was an equinox place, Mr. Stick had told her, where light and dark things were equally in power.

The brownstone was built in 1817 by a mason who never lived there, but who was later murdered and entombed in one of the house's walls. Its first longtime inhabitant was a spiritualist named Eleanor Cranch who was known for levitation, mothered twin daughters who spoke each other's thoughts, and eventually died of bone poisoning.

The house had often changed hands over the next century and a half, and because its inhabitants were usually secretive or downright hermetic, the place's full history was difficult to glean. Its various tenants and owners had included a prophetic artist, a warlock, a cult, a parapsychologist, an infamous herd of feral cats, and several people with no professed interest in the supernatural.

Mr. Stick had lived there alone for twenty-one years and had interacted with all manner of ghosts and beings. A dead baby whose immaterial form he couldn't cuddle, but whom he soothed with the colors of a vintage magic lantern. An invisible entity he called the Bishop, who did nothing but play chess extraordinary badly. Sentient paint that communicated via landscapes. A suicidal Venus flytrap. Grotesque and glorious creatures.

The brownstone's roof had once boasted a magnificent stone gargoyle, but it left. Meteorological phenomena regularly occurred indoors. Unfamiliar rooms would sometimes appear, and other rooms would move, disappear, or reconfigure. Mysteries deepened and compounded the more Mr. Stick learned and explored, and even after living there for two decades, he felt as if the house was hiding more than it was showing.

He told my mother about a spellbook made of elements—water, fire, earth, or air depending on the reader's need. Every now and then, the book was made of nothing. It had been found and lost a hundred times, and used in fabulous ways, but nobody who read it could remember what it said.

My mother's stories and my dreams squished together like Play-Doh. I asked her one night if all of it was true.

"How could I convince you?"

"Take me to the house," I said.

She laughed and shook her head: Yes and no, wish and warning.

"Have you seen anything weird?"

"All the time," my mother said.

"Like what?"

She smiled without changing expression, using the commonplace telepathy that she and I shared, and exhaled a soft breath that blanketed my chin.

"I've been talking to a ghost," she said.

I sat up in bed and asked her who it was, what they talked about, and loads of other questions in a rush, and when she finally had a chance to speak again, I didn't even notice that my first question—*who?*—was the one she didn't answer.

"We talk about the ways things are different after death. How life looks from this side and how it looks from *that* side. We talk about the fact that it's *possible* to talk."

She paused then, as if her thoughts had wandered out of time.

"After Poppy died," she said, referring to her father, "I looked for ways he might have been communicating with me. Do you remember how he'd sit in the kitchen with a coffee, absentmindedly tracing on the table with his finger?"

I didn't remember him doing that but nodded in agreement. I was young enough that nodding actually convinced me.

"He did it every day since I was *your* age," she said. "Traced a symbol like a six with an extra inner coil. I used to ask him what it was. He always said he didn't know and seemed surprised he was doing it.

"One winter night, a season after he died, there was the oddest sort of snow—like those pebbly little balls that come from broken Styrofoam. I was brushing off the car and you were in the backseat. You were four that year. You loved being inside the car and watching me appear whenever I brushed another window. Something about the way you laughed made me think of Poppy. I leaned over the windshield with the snowbrush and slipped. I cut my hand falling—I never figured out what I cut it on—and the blood made a swirly little six in the snow.

"When I stood up, you were laughing. You thought I'd fallen to be funny. But seeing the symbol had made me cry, and my crying made *you* start crying, and I hid my cut and got in the car and told you I was fine. They were happy tears, I said. I told you Poppy said hello."

"Poppy cut your hand?" I asked.

"No," my mother said. "I thought he used the blood. Then I thought I might have believed it just because I needed to."

"Have you talked to him in Mr. Stick's house?"

"I haven't but I'd like to. Anything can happen in a place like that." Then she laughed and said, "Everything I've seen, all the stories I've been sharing... I can't decide if Dad thinks I'm crazy or inventive."

I thought of what she'd said about needing to believe and how adults—my mother included—seemed to love having doubts.

"I think it's all real," I said.

"Sometimes the real things are harder to believe."

Then something happened during the night of February 26.

My mother had visited Mr. Stick early that evening and hadn't come home. I made my own cereal in the morning and took the bus to school, with a lunch prepared by my father and assurances that everything was fine.

It was a Thursday and I was especially daydreamy in the classroom, waiting for the heavy clouds to dump a load of snow. I didn't know until later that my father had taken the day off from work to locate my mother. He didn't know Mr. Stick's address—in the years that followed, he berated himself for taking so little interest in my mother's strange friend—and he began by calling the library where she worked. She hadn't arrived for the start of her shift, and none of her relatives or friends had heard from her in days. He checked the hospitals to no avail and was told by the police she hadn't been missing long enough to file a report.

He picked me up from school with tension in his eyes, as if the sockets in his skull were trying to contract.

"Why aren't we taking the bus?" I asked.

His silence scared me more than worry for my mother, who I honestly believed, at age seven, was immortal.

We arrived home to a ringing telephone. My father took the call, furrowed portions of his face I hadn't known were furrowable, and immediately packed me back into the car. My mother had been found in a secluded archival room of the library. No one had seen her enter the building that day, and since the room was off-limits to the public and rarely visited by the staff, she was discovered only when a young boy heard my mother talking. He'd thought she was a witch, her words were so peculiar.

One of the librarians—a friend of my mother's named Mrs. Janowski—investigated the room to ease the boy's mind. She found my mother reaching out and pushing at the air like a sleepwalker moving through a dream full of doors.

She didn't recognize us when we got to the library, and while my father checked her head for lumps or hidden blood, I stood aside and listened as she started mumbling nonsense. She talked about words people heard without ears. She spoke of closets full of loneliness, and bodies made of memories, and spaces you could mold like butter in your hands. Ghosts were everywhere, she said, and maybe we were *not*.

I watched my mother closely, afraid to be afraid, and hoped if I could understand everything she told us, it would mean that she was making sense and wasn't really crazy.

My father held her face and looked deeply into her eyes. "Where were you? Are you hurt?" he asked. "What happened last night?"

Her forehead crinkled like a burning sheet of paper.

"Night," she said. "Night…"

She concentrated hard but swirled around the word, as if recalling what had happened but confused about when.

"Ask Mr. Stick," she finally said. "He'll remember."

Mrs. Janowski leaned toward her, looking puzzled. "Leonard Stick?"

My mother half-smiled, half-nodded at the name.

Mrs. Janowski told my father, "Mr. Stick died a month ago. We went to his funeral together."

"She's been visiting him for weeks," my father said. "She's told us what they've talked about. She went to see him last night."

Mrs. Janowski shook her head. My father palmed his mouth.

Suddenly my mother felt light-years away, and she regarded me with a spectral sort of longing in her gaze, as if remembering my face instead of seeing me directly. The short gap between us felt impossible to cross.

"Mom?" I said.

I don't believe the sound reached her ears.

It was true: Mr. Stick had died a month earlier.

His obituary was brief, and all we eventually learned was that his funeral had been scantly attended and his body had been cremated. My father failed to locate any relatives or anyone who'd known him better than my mother. Mr. Stick's information had inexplicably vanished from the library database, and no trace of him existed in public records. Unable to learn his home address, neither my father nor the police could investigate his brownstone. It was as if the man's existence had been cremated with him.

Why my mother had gone to Mr. Stick's house after his death remained unexplained, but the fact that she'd behaved as if nothing was wrong indicated one of two things: either my mother had been keeping secrets for reasons unknown, or she'd been subtly losing her mind well before the night she went missing.

She was tested for concussion, stroke, tumor, drugs, and alcohol but appeared to be in perfect physical health. Her change was psychological, my father was informed, and so began months of tentative answers, treatments, and futility from various professionals, including therapists and priests, who taught us there are mysteries that nobody can plumb.

Her memory was scattershot. Her cognizance was warped. Certain times she knew us and began to feel like Mom again, but other times our faces sparked terror in her eyes, or flashes of euphoria, or unvoiced epiphany. Her life was dream and nightmare with hazes in between.

Some days, no one could penetrate the haze and she would sit at the living room window, breathing on the glass, convinced the snow was falling from the otherworld. Most days, it seemed as if the opposite were true and she was falling from the world and settling beyond us.

She would not—or could not—answer simple statements, or replied as if the statements had been something else entirely, or asked her own questions that defied understanding.

"Do you want a piece of cake?"
"Rooms are bodies when we're in them."

"Are you cold?"
"Three o'clock."

"I love you, Mom. It's me."
"What if the spiral wasn't hungry but expanded like a flower?"

My father was patient, loving, lost. He sat with her and held her hand. He cooked our meals, cleaned the house, and helped her in the bath. He steered their conversations, falling silent when she spoke to him in mysteries and riddles, and trying to guide her back to concrete memories and facts.

My mother was placid and easily cared for but my father refused to leave her alone for long periods of time. A friend of his suggested several nursing care options but my father wouldn't hear of it.

"She only needs some company," he said.

He found a new job and moved us two hundred miles away, into the middle of New England, where my mother's retired aunt could stay with her during the day.

I was lonely and generally friendless, a state of being that intensified in an unfamiliar school, where I spent my days preoccupied and tried to disappear. My withdrawal was so subtle, I was scarcely teased or bullied. My teachers didn't notice. Vanishing was easy.

At home in the evenings, I read books and comics next to my mother in the living room, predictably obsessed with supernatural material.

Sometimes my father put the television on and we would sit there and try to make a new kind of normal. He did his best to focus on her moments of lucidity, as if by ignoring her weird pronouncements and dementia he might, piece by piece, reconstruct the ordinary woman he remembered.

I saw her as I knew her, different but herself—a mother who chuckled when she sneezed, and hugged a lot, and daydreamed. I focused on her puzzling words and thought of them as clues, desperate to believe the mystery had meaning.

How else could I believe her when she told me that she loved me?

One night she came to my room and touched me out of sleep. Her eyes were oddly blue, like miniature jellyfish, and the rest of her was darker than the night should have made her.

"Mom?"

"Don't be scared."

I jolted up in bed.

"Shhh," my mother said. "I need to show you something important."

I relaxed at the soothing timbre of her voice, and once I'd settled back in bed, she almost seemed herself again—enough to make me wonder if she'd finally recovered.

"Close your eyes and cover your ears," she said, "and try to feel me standing here. Then see if you can recognize the difference when I'm gone. Will you do that for me?"

"OK," I said.

"Good."

I closed my eyes and covered my ears, distracted by my thoughts and peeking once or twice, and then I did my best to visualize her standing in the room. She was between the side of the bed, closer to the foot, and my battered wooden dresser, topped with books, against the wall. My nightlight had backlit the edges of her hair. The open door to the hallway was behind her to the right and if she backed away, five short steps, she'd be gone.

My nose had grown accustomed to her milk-and-nutmeg smell, and since I couldn't sense her bare feet moving on the floor, I trusted in the feeling she was teaching me to recognize. Her thereness and her beingness. Her room-filling motherness.

She'd given me a terrible task—to learn another way of feeling she was gone—and my heart beat heavier and sadder as I tried.

Hollowness emerged from the place she'd been standing. It was almost like the quiet after someone had been crying, or the space where a just-popped bubble had been floating. She'd softly left the room…or had I tricked myself with worry? I wanted to peek—I needed to know—but what if she was watching from the hall to see if I cheated, and all I wound up seeing was her disappointed face?

Instead of dwelling on the hollowness, I thought of how her closeness felt, summoning her near again and wishing it were true. Eventually I couldn't tell the difference anymore. I finally opened my eyes, with a hopeful kind of fear, and she was standing at my bedside just as she had been.

"I couldn't do it."

"Did you feel me here?"

"I thought I felt you leave."

"I did," my mother said, haloed by the nightlight. "But then I came back so you wouldn't feel alone."

Three weeks later, a full season after my mother had changed, I was drawn out of bed at 3 a.m., wearing green flannel pajamas, with the kind of mysterious purpose only children and somnambulists are wont to understand.

My father's distant snores harmonized with the refrigerator's hum. I walked down the hall and found my mother in the living room, sitting in her chair beside the window in the dark. She wasn't looking outside but faced me as I entered, and I crossed the carpet barefoot and stood in front of her chair.

She wiped her glassy eyes but only made them glassier.

"I dreamt that I was here and it was wonderful," she said. "I had bones and blood and fat and hair. My muscles changed shape underneath my skin. There were vibrating sounds, and colors I could touch, and if I pulled the air inside me, I could turn it into words."

I balled my fists, wishing she would simply be my mom again. I felt an urge to slap her, as people do in movies, and it made me feel queasy and demonic and adult. A parallelogram of light lay across her chest. The sky outside was moonless and the lamps weren't lit, and I was suddenly convinced the light was from a window that was hovering between us like a portal in the air.

She said, "I love you, William. Hold my hand."

I couldn't move my arms.

She was radiant but thin like a flame about to gutter. "I'll tell you something secret. Something you've forgotten. We choose a way forward, at the start and at the end. It's time for me to choose again. It's time for me to go."

I felt the space broadening and shadowing around us, and a cold, prickling updraft floated from the floor. She reached her hand toward me with an upturned palm, and since I didn't have pockets in the pants of my pajamas, I slid my hands deep beneath the tight elastic waistband and held my own legs. They were goosefleshed and skinny.

A pine scent, evergreen and gray, wafted off her.

My eyes focused hard on anything but her. Her chair's stout legs stood firmly in the carpet. The radiator's heavy old bulk looked cold, with a skin of white paint over thick, scaly rust, and the window was as black as volcanic glass.

My mother lowered her hand but kept it open on her knee.

When I looked at her again, the parallelogram had risen and

was covering her face like pale, electric water. Light filled her eyes. She flowered with relief, as if she'd lost me in a crowd and suddenly caught a glimpse. She whispered something.

"Mom?"

"*Look*," my mother said.

I didn't whirl around but gazed into her eyes, expecting some telepathy of everything inside her: spectral rooms and vistas, winged and crawling creatures, multicolored fire, eclipses and auroras and, most of all, beautiful and terrifying spirits— wearing dresses, rags, uniforms, smoke, or rippling light—with the stories of their lives and deaths drifting on their faces like kaleidoscopes of sun and shade in windy, cloudy weather.

Instead I saw my mother's ghost, naked and translucent, sitting in the chair and doubling her body. I wasn't yet crying so it couldn't have been my tears, and I wouldn't have imagined seeing her undressed. I knew what I was seeing right away and I believed it. All I'd ever felt from her as long as I'd existed—the color of her closeness, in her body and her sight, and everything that made her Mom—was visible and pure.

The parallelogram of light wavered and dissolved.

My mother's ghost vanished.

Then her body in the chair was like the window and the radiator—tangible and dead and awfully, darkly real. The tiny black pupils in her irises were empty. They were holes.

When I looked inside, no one looked back.

In the years after she died, my father refused to credit any supernatural power, insisting she had suffered an undetectable brain injury and raising me in a flood of practical precautions. He'd lost his wife to bodily harm. He wouldn't lose me. He gave me bike helmets; swimming lessons; warnings about drugs, sex, and strangers; first-aid courses; and, when I was old enough to drive, a sturdy car and strategies for every sort of hazard.

"If there's a deer in the road and no time to stop, what do you do?"

"Swerve," I said.

"Wrong. You're liable to hit a tree or oncoming traffic. Hit the deer but take your foot off the brakes before impact. Brakes lower the car and make it likelier the deer will crash through your windshield."

"I couldn't kill a deer."

"Better it than you."

He said it gently, though, and sadly, as he did whenever he talked about catastrophe and death. The world was flesh and sticks, he thought, and minimizing breakage was the best we could hope for.

"I'd swerve and save the deer," I said, "*and* avoid crashing."

"It isn't worth the risk. Save your own life first. It's all you'll ever have and it's important to protect it."

"Would you risk yourself for me?"

He sighed from a place much deeper than his lungs. "Of course I would, William. That's a whole different thing."

We talked about my mother a lot, focusing on her life. But there were bounds to what the two of us would share about our grief, especially as our everyday outlooks diverged. He never openly discouraged my ongoing interest in the occult—throughout my childhood and adolescence, he paid for any book, magazine, TV-advertised encyclopedia of the unknown, sinister record, movie, artifact, or mail-order specimen I wanted—but I knew he always viewed it all as therapeutic play.

Exploring the occult mollified my loneliness and gave me spectral lenses everywhere I went. I saw meaning in random symbols, in the movements of insects and birds, in the gaps between songs I listened to at night, and in the books no one else my age seemed to read. Secrets were a fingernail scratch below the surface. My mother, I believed, was close enough to touch if only I could hit upon the right way to reach.

I meditated. I prayed. I hypnotized myself so deeply that I achieved, through self-suggestion, the ability to speak an unidentified language for three and a half hours—a language I believed my mother could hear but didn't answer.

I took Polaroids of empty spaces whenever I sensed another presence, and although the film captured luminous orbs and smudges, and one time a fully-formed, ghostly male body, I never managed to photograph a glimmer of my mother.

I looked for her in Tarot spreads and saw nothing but myself.

I used a Ouija board with a bone planchette. I made fleeting contact with many different entities, most of whom confined themselves to yes-or-no answers, and almost befriended one nervous spirit of undetermined gender until he or she, like everyone in my life, went away without explanation.

One night in winter, I took a knife outside and crunched across the yard. The snow had partially melted during the day, and the surface had refrozen into a thin crust of ice. My boots left a trail of foot-shaped holes. Fresh snow was in the air and somehow the atmosphere prevented it from settling. It whirled around and hovered, rising up as much as falling. In the dark rear of the yard, I held the blade against my hand. I shut my eyes, visualized my mother sitting in her chair, and made a quick, bright cut across the middle of my palm.

I waited for the flow to start and flung my hand downward. I made a fist and opened my eyes, and there was just enough light to see the splatter on the ice. My boots had broken through to the softer snow below, and I stood a long time, sunken to my calves, until it felt as if my feet were frozen underground.

No matter how I tried interpreting the pattern, the blood looked meaningless on the ground.

One night when I was seventeen, my father walked into my room and caught me getting drunk.

"I want to talk to her again," I said.

"You will."

"You don't believe that."

He picked up the pint of vodka, two-thirds gone, I'd tried to hide on the floor behind me when he'd entered. I pushed the bottle away. He finished it off, took a breath, and looked at me intensely.

"I trick myself," he said, "believing there's an afterlife. It helps me live. It helps me not remember that I'll die someday. What's strange is that the older I get, the more I really believe it—that there's something after everything. It isn't just nothing."

"I know. I've talked to ghosts," I said, electrified—and buzzed—that he'd finally broached the subject we had tacitly agreed never to discuss.

"That isn't what I mean," he said.

"I've done it, though," I told him. "I just haven't found a way to contact Mom."

He threw the empty bottle against the wall and it exploded. I flinched and kept my head down, feeling twin urges to apologize and shove him.

"I love you, William. Look at me."

He stared at me so long, I had to stare back. I smelled the vodka in the air and saw the whiskers on his jaw, and he was real and fake and vaporous and solid all together.

"Even if you're right and people live forever," he said, "sometimes you're going to have to let things go."

I was twenty-five years old the night my father died. He was driving on a rural road, next to a cemetery of all places, and collided with a maple tree. His airbag failed and the crash killed him instantly.

A witness said he swerved to avoid a crossing deer.

He was buried next to my mother with a simple granite headstone bearing both their names. On the day of his interment, I sat alone at the gravesite after the mourners and diggers had gone, wondering if my parents were together or apart, or if the best they'd ever have was neighboring in dirt.

I was living in a one-room apartment at the time, rarely dating or socializing, and drifting through the kinds of anonymous temp jobs afforded to someone with an online degree in Occult and Mystical Esoterica. My father left me everything, including a significant life insurance payout, and in the weeks after he died, I stopped accepting temp assignments and spent all of my time at his house eating the food he'd never eat, packing up his things, and feeling like the ghost of a once-living family.

I found a duct-taped box he probably hadn't opened in a decade. Inside was a small but carefully curated selection of my mother's belongings, including love letters from my father, her favorite cable-knit sweater, my own baby teeth, and a handful of books.

I flipped through her copy of *The Spiral Grimoire*, a little-known but fascinating assortment of rituals and spells. I inhaled the old-book fragrance I'd forever associate with my librarian mother and discovered her handwriting on the flyleaf.

She'd written, "L. Stick," along with an address.

2. THE BEDROOM GHOST

My father's death made sense. I had visited the crash site, seen the trees along the road, and spotted several deer walking in the woods. I wasn't at all surprised he'd swerved to save a deer because it fit the man I'd known—one who'd cared for me and my mother and hadn't, despite his advice, put his own life before anybody else's. I missed him and I grieved, but his death had given me answers.

My mother's death had left questions. Now with Mr. Stick's address, I could visit where she'd gone and learn what had happened. If the building was as special as my mother had described, I might be able to do what I'd failed to do at home: speak with her directly one last time and finally make sense of how and why I'd lost her.

I learned that Mr. Stick's former home belonged to a woman named Mrs. Zabka, a widow of late-middle age whom I was able to reach by phone.

Mrs. Zabka was a shut-in, and although she declined my invitation to visit her in person, she was a friendly conversationalist, happy to answer my questions and, when I probed too deeply, polite in her refusal to divulge information.

She had acquired ownership of the brownstone from Mr. Stick a week before his death, which he had apparently known was imminent, and she even remembered speaking to my mother on one occasion.

"I liked her," Mrs. Zabka said. "I was sorry to hear what happened."

"What *did* happen?" I asked.

"Heavens, who can say? I never understood the place or most of what occurs there."

I tried to engage her on the subject of her brownstone's otherworldliness, mentioning some of the marvels and phenomena my mother had told me about, and Mrs. Zabka listened like a woman who believed or was simply too mannerly to baldly contradict me. I talked too long about my academic interest in the occult, trying to convince her I wasn't a lunatic or quack, and then abruptly shifted to a personal appeal.

"I'm still haunted by my mother. By the mystery," I said, "and not just the loss. I realize how off-putting all of this might be, but I'd like to see your house and spend some time exploring, if only so the place itself isn't such a mystery."

"You're coming to a haunted house to stop feeling haunted."

"That's a good way to say it. So you do think it's haunted?"

"I can promise you'll encounter more than you expect, but I can't guarantee it's haunted by your mother."

"If I can't find my mother, I'll try to find closure."

"You might find a whole new opening," she said.

"I'd appreciate the chance more than I can say. I'm happy to compensate you for letting me visit."

"You could live there," she said, "exploring all you like."

She told me she was willing to sell the house, and had in fact been waiting years for an appropriate buyer—someone who understood the brownstone's nature and wouldn't balk at the stack of legal disclosures, failed inspections, decrepitude, and warnings. Given her shut-in status, I was surprised she wanted to move.

"Oh, I've never lived there," Mrs. Zabka said.

She was an absentee owner, residing in the suburbs, and hadn't visited the place in the years since Mr. Stick died.

"May I ask why you bought it?"

"Someone needs to own it."

"Has anyone maintained it?"

"The house maintains itself," she said.

Years of study and experience had taught me there was more than one kind of ghost. Some were caring. Some were violent. Some were grieving, scared, or lost. There were conscious ghosts who interacted with the living, and there were others who were more like residues or echoes—perceptible but totally unable to perceive.

What they all had in common was a tether to the world. Whatever the links or reasons, they were here instead of gone.

When my mother had left Mr. Stick's house only partially herself, maybe part of her had stayed. Would she talk or be an echo? At very least, the house itself was bound to give me answers, and I was more than willing to face whatever dangers might exist if I could finally escape the limbo of unknowns.

I moved into my new home on a feverish January day that started off sunny and ended—auspiciously, I thought—with a squall producing thundersnow. Being immediately housebound because of the storm didn't worry me, since I had already arranged for reliable grocery deliveries, I had no local friends or family to visit, and I had no intention of leaving the house after waiting so long to thoroughly explore it.

The building was an abnormally narrow but otherwise unremarkable brownstone, wedged like a shim between a pair of other brownstones. There was no house number, no baroque doorknocker, and no uncanny chill produced by its appearance. The chocolate-brick façade featured an oak door on the first story and skinny twin windows on each of the two upper floors. The neighboring buildings abutted mine directly and allowed for no side windows in the front two-thirds of the house. In the rear, however, my brownstone extended fully to the alley and the neighboring buildings didn't, leaving space on either side and a smattering of windows that offered light and limited views.

My house's slenderness contrasted with its extraordinary depth, which made the interior feel simultaneously claustrophobic and endless. Its hallways ran lengthwise but zigzagged at intervals, with the doorways to rooms alternating sides, and so it was impossible to stand in the front and look directly to the rear. The layout was nook-like, many-cornered, and disorienting. A child playing hide and seek could disappear for hours.

The entire building smelled of burnt cinnamon, except for my second-story bedroom, which smelled of warm spring mist. No actual mist was perceptible but the window overlooking the street was fogged with heavy moisture. I had a bed, a nightstand, a dresser, and a lamp, along with a small and tidy bathroom next to the bedroom closet.

The house contained a comfortable study, a formal dining room, an additional bathroom, innumerable closets and compartments, and many other rooms, both major and minor, that were connected in semi-logical ways and enticed me with unique personalities and auras.

And yet for all the promising character, nothing otherworldly revealed itself during my initial walkthrough, and shortly after dusk, with the January slush-light of sunset around me, I wondered if the house distrusted me. I was new, after all—as foreign to the building as the building was to me. Maybe the house was keeping secrets in the presence of a stranger.

Over the years, I'd found that undressing in unfamiliar places—hotel rooms, for instance, or long-neglected burial grounds—fostered greater openness and trust in my environment. My body was so compounded with my identity that physical nakedness seemed to expose my truest self. And while my vulnerability was largely symbolic—a necktie and pants hadn't made me safer, especially since paranormal dangers were more liable to threaten my sanity and spirit—I *felt* more at risk without the armor of my clothes.

I undressed that night and walked around naked, wearing only my shoes because of the nails and broken glass in several of the rooms. I hoped the house would recognize my gesture of unguardedness. Desperate for any sign of life, I re-explored the whole building, listening and watching, and then I brushed off a chair in the dining room and sat beneath the unlit chandelier. I thought I heard the dust motes settling around me.

"Hello?" I said.

The dark offered nothing in reply.

"Hello," I said again, answering myself.

I gathered my clothes and carried them up to my twilit bedroom, missing my parents and disappointed that my new home hadn't presented so much as a ghostly twinkle or unexplained creak.

Upstairs, the bedroom's tropical warmth soothed my chill from the otherwise wintry house, and I was prepared to sleep naked, as I might have done in summer, when I suddenly felt what seemed to be a breath inside my ear.

I spun. The room was empty. Nevertheless I felt the rising

shame of standing there naked. My sense of being watched seemed to indicate a watcher.

I snatched a sheet to cover myself. I'd made my bed less than two hours earlier, and yet in the interval a spider's nest, apparently hidden in the mattress, had spectacularly hatched. Dozens of grape-sized spiders polka-dotted the bed and scattered chaotically as soon as I exposed them. Many clung to the sheet I'd wrapped around my waist, and both my penis and my thighs were overrun with tickles.

I clutched the sheet and laughed. There I'd been, glum and lonely in the moribund house, and now a panoply of spiders and a ghost had appeared.

"Hello!" I said, thrilling at the animated room.

I swapped the sheet for flannel pajamas and sat on a narrow, spiderless section of the bed, and then I closed my eyes and covered my ears, exactly as my mother had taught me as a child.

I had encountered ghosts before but only passingly. I'd rarely felt the true, electric sparkle of connection. Generally ghosts regarded me with hazy apprehension, as if the skin between our worlds were too opaque to see through. Contact was often like a flashlight through a hand when only the glow and maybe a vein or two are easily discerned.

This was something else.

I sensed the ghost was female. She stood in the corner of the bedroom, slightly to my right, watching me and radiating needful curiosity. A D-minor tone persisted in my hearing like a pressure change, or possibly a memory of sadness, and I couldn't tell if she or I—or both of us—was causing it.

"Hello," I said. "I'm William. Do you live here, too?"

She faded like a cellphone signal in a tunnel. I concentrated hard and leaned in her direction but a growing void of loneliness convinced me she was gone.

I opened my eyes and stared at the empty corner, where a hook and wire dangled from the rough brick wall. An earlier inhabitant had probably hung a picture there. I felt the ghost's absence like I felt the missing picture.

I shooed the remaining spiders onto the floor and lay in bed. "Someone's in my house," I thought. "Possibly a friend."

I woke the next morning with a cobwebby head, but once I wiped the silk out of my hair and eyes, my bedroom felt common again, aside from the strange humidity and an odd cast of light that had followed me out of a dream.

"Hello?" I said.

The bedroom ghost was nowhere to be felt but I began the day with a reborn sense of possibility. I dressed in jeans, an Oxford shirt, and a necktie—a uniform that placed me in the relaxed professional mindset of someone comfortable at work—and walked downstairs to the kitchen. I remembered the brownstone's original builder was entombed inside the house, and for reasons I couldn't articulate, I strongly suspected his bones were in the wall behind the refrigerator.

The fridge itself was avocado green and had the kind of latch-handle door, outlawed since the Refrigerator Safety Act of 1956, that contributed to the deaths of curious children who accidentally locked themselves in. I started a pot of coffee and imagined, as it brewed, what it would feel like to suffocate alone inside a box. Just as clearly, I imagined being the skeleton in the wall.

When the coffee was ready, I carried the carafe and my favorite orange mug up to the second-floor study. This was a large, rectangular room in the rear of the house with two windows, decrepit brick walls, and a heavy plank floor that had been smoothed, by two centuries of footfalls, to creamy warm softness.

I had an oriental rug the color of bread mold, a simple but imposing work desk, a trio of bookcases, a small stereo with a turntable, an upholstered reading chair, and seventeen unopened boxes of books, bones, candles, talismans, phials, records, vintage occult instruments, notebooks, and ballpoint pens: everything required to make the study my center of operations.

I had scarcely unpacked the first box of supplies when I noticed a fluttery shadow in my periphery and turned to the window. A pigeon had landed on the sill. He tilted his head and watched me with a keen, beady eye and I approached the window slowly, happy for the company. His body was unusually thick, especially in the back, and I thought without judgment that he must be a glutton.

When the pigeon flew off, I discovered my mistake. His burliness hadn't been fat but rather an extra folded wing. I opened the sash and stuck my head outside, startled by the sparkling cold and thrilled to see the three-winged pigeon flap away. The extra wing was on his right side and made him fly erratically. I watched him enter a leafless tree, tangle in the limbs, and extricate himself before he ascended over a neighboring house and fluttered out of sight.

An omen, I believed, of prodigies to come.

I wasn't disappointed. Prodigies abounded.

One morning, I discovered my dining room was coated with an ultrafine layer of snow. The table, floor, and wrought-iron chandelier were lunar white when I entered, and I assumed the powder was dust until I wiped the table with my palm.

The sensation was painfully cold but oddly refreshing, like peppermint absorbed directly into my skin.

According to a thermometer I fetched from my study, the dining room was eight degrees Fahrenheit despite an otherwise well-heated building and a working radiator in the dining room itself. When the localized cold began to disperse, I swept as much of the snow as possible into a Mason jar. The snow soon melted into seventeen ounces of water, and yet the water remained unnaturally cold. I was strongly tempted to drink it but ultimately placed the jar in my curiosities closet, where I discovered, in the shadows, that the water was faintly luminous.

Another day, the water in the house's pipes became impossibly hot—well beyond boiling point without becoming steam. A one-minute flow not only deformed the kitchen faucet but raised the room's temperature so dramatically I fainted from the heat.

When I revived and fled to the cooler hallway, I heard a deep, metallic groaning in the downstairs bathroom. The sound was coming from the pipes, which were bowing and distending from the superheated water. I ran the sink and bathtub faucets to relieve the strain but succeeded only in damaging the drain pipes, too.

I ran from the bathroom to the first-floor utility room. My ancient hot-water tank was oily black and massive, with heavily grimed gauges, knobs, and valves, like a repurposed boiler from an evil locomotive. A flaking label read DO NOT ADJUST. I twisted several unmarked dials, then kicked the tank to quiet an ominous rumble. Nothing appeared out of order, and when I returned to the bathroom and retried the faucets, the water's temperature had already begun to drop.

Much of my plumbing was visible along the house's exposed brick walls and the lasting damage was immediately apparent. Horizontal pipes had sagged. Vertical pipes had tapered and bulged like hideous balloon animals. There were blockages and leaks, and from that day forward, the pipes' distorted widths caused my toilet to flush with breathtaking suction and my faucets to dribble or spurt with unpredictable force.

My radiators sounded like a choir of murdered children, and now and then I sat and listened, wondering if the house was threatening me. Yet the radiators' song was balefully lovely and the distorted pipes lent a grotesque but singular aesthetic to the walls. The house, evolving in my presence, felt more and more like home.

A different sort of mystery came to light when I visited the basement.

One dirty lightbulb with a pull chain lit the area near the stairs, and I used my pocketlight to illuminate my way around the darker depths and grottos. Motes swarmed the air but the air felt dead. The space was loaded with support beams, cobwebs, discarded furniture, moldering crates, broken tools, and dust-furred debris. All told, it was an especially decrepit but otherwise typical old basement. The ceiling joists were low and flooring nails jabbed downward only inches over my scalp. The walls were irregular concrete, studded with rocks and bricks and rusted metal, and several partial collapses of the foundation had been reinforced with makeshift buttresses.

The floor was also concrete, with cracks, swells, oily puddles, mounds of dirt, and powdery efflorescence. Much of the floor's rear half was a patchwork of iron plates, welded trapdoors, and wooden platforms weighted down with boxes and scrap metal.

In the northeast corner, I illuminated a curious tableau. A black iron safe was riveted to the floor. The safe was three foot square, with an imposing handle and a combination lock, and was surrounded by what appeared to be a child's furniture set. There was a tiny chair, a miniature table, and a steel-framed cot the length of my leg. On the table stood a coffee mug and a stalagmite of wax with an unlit, semi-melted candle on top. Beside the cot was a small wooden radio, the dial of which was tuned to my favorite station.

The radio played when I switched it on. The candlewax was pliably fresh. After determining the safe was locked, I went upstairs to call Mrs. Zabka on the phone and ask her if she knew the combination.

Mrs. Zabka informed me that everything in the northeast corner of the basement belonged to a man named Mr. Gormly. He alone, she assured me, knew the combination. When I asked who Mr. Gormly was and where he'd gone after abandoning his possessions, she said the man had lived in the basement for decades and, as far as she understood, was living there still.

I was astonished by the news and asked her why I hadn't been informed about him earlier. Mrs. Zabka corrected me: I had been informed when I read and signed Addendum 7c of the Affidavit of Title, which guaranteed Mr. Gormly's right to inhabit the northeast corner of the basement in perpetuity. She assured me Mr. Gormly was a quiet tenant who paid his rent, in cash, on the night of each new moon.

That explained the mint-scented envelope, containing a hundred-dollar bill, I'd found in my study the day I moved in. I had assumed some previous inhabitant had left the bill behind.

"This is fantastic," I said. "He must have known my mother and Mr. Stick. Decades in the house—imagine what he's seen and everything he knows! I've got to introduce myself as soon as possible."

"No one's ever seen him."

"How does he live down there with nothing but child-sized furniture?"

"He must be very small," Mrs. Zabka said.

"But what does he eat and drink? How does he come and go?"

"That's not for me to say. In fact, I don't know."

Needless to say, I was eager to meet my mysterious tenant and speak with him directly. When I failed to encounter Mr. Gormly on subsequent trips to the basement, I resigned myself to waiting for the next new moon, when he would emerge to pay his rent, and tried not to take his apparent indifference to me personally.

The bedroom ghost was elusive, too.

I tried and failed to summon her with necromantic incantations, she didn't speak via Ouija, and I was unwilling to perform any sacrificial rituals, not only for ethical reasons but also because she hadn't seemed the type—or rather I hoped she wasn't the type—who needed such inducements to interact.

I thought I sensed her sometimes, in a variety of ways. A sudden fascination with a corner of my bedroom, starting as an absentminded, daydreamy gaze that turned into certainty that somebody was there. A multihued scent I couldn't quite name, like a link between otherwise unrelated memories. A fluctuating ringing in my blood-flushed ear.

Was I growing more attuned to hints of her existence, or was she growing more adept at making herself known? I often closed my eyes, covered my ears, and tried to feel her out. I spoke to her at night and waited patiently for answers. In the meantime, I explored the house, spent hours with my books studying other ways to contact the dead, and worried I had imagined her to counteract my loneliness.

One morning I woke and discovered a symbol, like a small crescent moon, had been drawn on the fogged glass of my bedroom window. There were three possibilities:

The ghost had attempted physical communication.

Someone—Mr. Gormly?—had entered my room while I was sleeping and written on the window.

I had sleepwalked and drawn the symbol myself.

Heartened, puzzled, and disturbed in equal measure, I dressed and went to the kitchen, where I mulled the symbol's meaning and appearance. I ate a banana mashed with cinnamon, drank a cup of coffee, and returned to my bedroom with an idea.

Under the symbol on the glass, I wrote a little question mark.

Then I sat on the bed, sucked a cough drop, and waited for an hour in a meditative state. Eventually I went to my study to read a treatise called Fuliginous Semiology, hoping to expand my communication options with ethereal entities. Books were good friends that never disappeared, and yet for all their personality and telepathic strength—the ability of an author to speak to me directly, on demand, over time and space—the relationship was limited to what a book gave. I wanted to be needed back. I wanted conversation.

I struggled to concentrate because of my preoccupation with the ghost and, it must be said, my only halfhearted interest in the language of smoke. I went to my bedroom in the late afternoon with slumped expectations. My natural introversion, coupled with years of stillborn relationships, had led me to begrudgingly accept lonely solitude. I'd learned to fear connection as much as I craved it, avoiding bars and cafes and even social media, because the more I wanted contact, the more I felt its absence. This interminable loop afflicted me that day, and I entered my bedroom with the intention of wiping my question mark off the foggy glass, and with it any chance of further disappointment.

The ghost was in the room.

I immediately sensed her just beside the window, where she had traced a clumsy squiggle in the corner of the glass. The squiggle's meaninglessness was moot. She'd returned. She had tried.

I walked to the window and stood next to her, happy to sense she didn't disappear or move away. I wiped the window clean—the moisture felt warm but the glass felt cold—and then I leaned down and refogged the surface with my breath.

"Tabula rasa," I said, feeling inwardly and outwardly the blankness of potential.

It seemed as if my whole day alone hadn't happened. I drew a short mark, like the squiggle she had left me. Then I sidestepped, giving her room to stand in front of the window, and she drew a fresh line in answer to my own. Our squiggles intersected as a lowercase *t*. The point at which they crossed was intimately lovely with a teardrop of moisture clinging to the glass, exactly where our fingertips had alternately touched.

I wrote the word "William" above the "t" and moved aside again.

She took three minutes to write her own name. Her invisible finger trembled from the concentrated effort, and she paused after each completed letter—and sometimes mid-letter—like a person forced to write in an unaccustomed way. I imagined writing with my foot, or with a string instead of a pen. With each slow mark she made on the glass, I saw the evidence of care, doggedness, and need.

The finished word was poorly formed but wonderfully distinct.

I read her name aloud and she immediately vanished.

One second she'd felt closer to me than ever, the next she'd disappeared without a hint of explanation. Had writing on the glass depleted her somehow, or was she so akin to me—introverted, fearful of her craving to connect—that merely sharing her name had forced her to retreat?

I stared at what we'd written.

William

+

June

3.STRANGE COMPANY

The three-winged pigeon returned to my study's windowsill every morning at exactly 9 a.m.

His punctuality may not have been preternatural but rather a perfect inner clock attuned to daily sunlight. His reliable visits mollified my loneliness, and I began to pause in my habitual reading at precisely 8:59 a.m. to witness his arrival.

Why did he come? What did he want? He was an ordinary rock dove, pale gray with black-barred wings and an iridescent purple throat, in every way normal except for his extra limb. I admired his strange beauty and, as many people do in their relationships with animals, began to assume a degree of rapport that may have been imagined.

One morning before his arrival, I opened the sash and placed a bowl of sunflower seeds on the ledge. A blade of winter air cut across my ankles while I waited in my reading chair.

The pigeon landed in an anarchy of wings and scrabbling claws, a sudden fluttery mess that rapidly resolved to elegance and calm. He cocked his head and looked at me. I cocked my head back.

The pigeon ignored the bowl at first, seemingly enchanted by the window's open sash and relishing how the house's warmth breezed through his feathers. He stepped toward the room and I wondered with excitement if he might decide to enter. Instead he looked at me a while, neither inside nor out, and my thoughts swayed poetically to thresholds and portals.

At 9:03 a.m., he nudged the sunflower seeds brusquely with his beak, ruffled his neck, and flew away, leaving the window and the room emptier and colder.

Likewise, June kept visiting and vanishing. I wrote simple messages on my bedroom window—"Good Morning", "Who Are You?"—but she either refused to answer or had lost the ability to do so.

Still I sensed her in my room once or twice a day. Whenever she was near, I greeted her aloud, wrote on the window, or tried new ways to get her to communicate. I blew out candles to see if she could manipulate the coils of rising smoke. I held a pen to a notebook and cleared my mind, hoping she'd possess me into automatic writing. Nothing helped, nothing worked. She intensified and faded like a drawing under tracing paper. At times she felt close—an onion skin away—and then the layer grew between us and she blurred or disappeared.

One night in February, I made a gut-wrenching discovery.

June had been completely absent for half a week and I had ceased to look for her return. I'd assumed she was choosing to avoid me or had simply lost interest, and the rejection had almost put me off trying to contact other spirits, encounter Mr. Gormly, or care about the pigeon visiting my study.

The house had accepted me fully by then, presenting a steady array of wondrous or disquieting phenomena, but that particular day was mostly uneventful, and even the blinding light that strobed for eight minutes from the downstairs toilet was a disappointing substitute for personal interaction. I left my study just before midnight, took a shower, and entered my bedroom naked. Despite my room's humid warmth, a mild fever had left me with a chill, and I walked to my secondary storage closet for an extra blanket.

When I opened the closet door, I felt a strange, quavering air in the narrow dark space. I'd opened the closet four days earlier and encountered nothing unusual, and so I backed away and pondered the peculiar new atmosphere.

I realized it was June. Several seconds passed before she rushed out of the closet and moved directly into me. I felt a flood of empathy and mutual possession as our lonelinesses blended in a saturating hug. Just as quickly, she was through me and behind me in the room. I crouched and cried—wept is more exact—not only from the wine-drunk sadness she'd infused me with, but also from the body-wide loss of our communion. We'd been thoroughly together. We were thoroughly apart again.

I pressed my spine against the doorjamb, head between my knees, and waited for my breathing and my tears to settle down.

She'd been locked inside the closet, possibly for days. Had she materialized there and found herself trapped, or had I locked her in myself earlier that week? Either way, opening the door had proved impossible to a ghost who could barely trace her name. She'd been as hopelessly confined as a child in a latching fridge.

I stood and crossed the room, turning off the lamp so the only illumination came from a streetlight glowing down the block, and quickly got dressed in boxers and an undershirt.

I sensed June's presence more easily than ever. Passing through me, she had left me with a tinge of who she was, as if we'd kissed and I could still taste the flavor of her toothpaste, or as if the two of us had talked all night and I could recognize her voice days later in a crowd.

She hid between the bed and the wall, near the nightstand

corner with the tumbleweed dust. She filled the air as tangibly as worry in my chest. Instead of touching her again, I sat beside her on the floor and hoped my mere companionship would give her reassurance.

Her terrible ordeal had raised many questions.

If she could vanish from the bedroom any time she chose, why had she remained imprisoned in the closet?

She couldn't drift through walls, so how had she drifted through my body?

Assuming she could walk and sit, did gravity affect her?

How much of her was physical? How much of her was not?

I let my thoughts float and focused on her mood. Her electrical panic seemed to disperse, and eventually she moved and lay on the bed above me, watching me—I think—and comforted to have me there.

She seemed to fall asleep. I hoped she could dream.

I fell asleep, too. In the morning she was gone but I could feel the way she'd moved underneath my skin.

In early March, a new door appeared in my house. It was located in an unfurnished bedroom on the third floor and I confirmed—by studying photos from my realtor—the door didn't exist when I bought the house in December.

The room's plaster walls were painted a shade best described as abandoned-hospital green. Chunks of plaster had broken off, revealing the underlying brick. The room was small and dim. There was a single wooden chair.

When I entered the room from the hallway, the mysterious new door was centered in the wall to my right. The frame was six feet tall and two feet wide, and the door itself was roughhewn wood of an unknown species. The wood smelled of incense and midwinter wreaths, the way a temple door smells after decades of worship.

I opened the door toward me with a black iron ring pull.

The sight of myself beyond the door made me jump backward. My reflection jumped, too, but not with perfect symmetry. I stared at myself, observing how my self stared back, and then the two of us seemed to realize there were two of us indeed.

The doorway wasn't a mirror. It was a passage to another room, identical to mine, in which a whole Other William looked at me, amazed.

Was *he* an Other William or was *I* an Other William? Had I summoned him by opening the door, or had he summoned me by opening a door in his own equivalent brownstone? Judging by my twin's fascinated squint, he was puzzling over the same perspectival conundrum.

Twice we started to talk at precisely the same moment, then stopped to listen when we realized the other was speaking. I sat in the wooden chair, determined to converse with him. Other William did the same.

"Who are you?" I asked.

"I'm William Rook."

"So am I."

We heard and saw each other clearly, which meant that soundwaves and light could pass between our rooms and yet I suspected, with primal anxiety, that to bodily cross the threshold would court annihilation.

"If you tell me you're real," Other William said, "it's either true and I won't believe you—because how can it possibly be true?—or it's false and I'm delusional."

"What if both of us are real and both of us believe it?"

"Ask me, then," he said.

I straightened and inhaled. He slumped and held his breath.

"Are you real?" I asked.

"Yes."

"Maybe we're hallucinating."

"If we're both hallucinations, there would have to be a third me. An actual hallucinator."

I nodded and paused, acknowledging his good sense and feeling a strange sort of pride, as when I sometimes visualized myself as very wise. I wanted to impress him with an intelligent response, and I gave the matter an extra minute of consideration, knowing only a fool would consciously shortchange himself.

"We'll talk about ourselves," I said. "I'll tell you everything I did today, in the finest possible detail, including what led me to open this door. When I'm finished, you'll do the same."

"What will that accomplish?" Other William asked.

"It's easier to recognize a truth-teller once you get him talking."

"Or a liar."

Coming from anyone else, his persistent contrariness might have irked me, and yet his voice and even his thoughts were wonderfully familiar and I felt a kind of deep mental calm as we conversed.

I recounted every part of my day: my morning coffee and cinnamon banana; the four accounts of ravenous ghosts I'd read in the study; my exploration of the oddments room; the fingertip I'd accidentally severed; the reattachment of my fingertip using skinwort; the levitating squirrel; and the irresistible urge, beginning at 3 p.m., to visit the current room for no particular reason.

"Five accounts," he said.

I realized he was right: I'd forgotten the dullest account of ravenous ghosts, but Other William had apparently read the same stories that morning and both of us remembered all five when he corrected me.

"We had the same day," I said.

"Which proves you're in my head," Other William answered. "My brain created you and didn't even bother to get imaginative."

"Or we're doppelgängers living identical lives, in identical brownstones, on opposite sides of the doorway."

"Then shouldn't we be opposites?"

"Mirrorlike," I said. "Equivalent but backwards."

"Is one of us evil?"

"I don't think so. But you strike me as a pessimist."

"And you're an optimist," he said with subtle condescension.

"We're a literal split personality. It's marvelous."

"And chilling."

We were restless then, as eager to do something else as anyone after intense self-reflection, and we agreed to separate for the time being and independently research our encounter before we met again.

I smiled. He did not. We said goodbye and closed the doors.

Walking away from myself left me viscerally disassociated, as if I'd floated out of my body as a whole second body. I was hyperaware that everything about me, from my tiniest movements to my thoughts, was being mirrored by myself in some identical reality. At first I felt doubly self-conscious, but my embarrassment seemed more in line with Other William's negative demeanor, and so I shifted my perspective and began to feel positive and doubly alive. I was twice as active, twice as hopeful, twice as me.

I wanted to share my experience with someone other than

myself and went to my bedroom, hoping June was there. She wasn't in the room.

I wrote, "I need you," in the window fog and felt twice as lonely.

A house is haunted only by the people who are in it.

My small square kitchen, with its familiar cabinets, cans of soup, and Mr. Coffee, was normally a room of nourishment and comfort. Then one night alone, I entered and found the space inexplicably smudged with sadness. The ceiling fixture's bulbs glowed like failing candles and a sorrow from the past—from within the kitchen itself, or from a corner of my childhood?—seeped into the present like color through a bandage.

The three-winged pigeon continued to visit my study's windowsill. I tried offering pumpkin seeds, corn kernels, breadcrumbs, cranberries, maggots, pine nuts, granola, and jackfruit, but the pigeon rejected them all. Every day, he perched and watched me with an unexplained intensity. There was something crazed and focused in the pigeon's staring eye, conveying both inquisitiveness and imminent attack. I wished he would eat. I wished he would trust me.

I put off revisiting my doppelgänger, not yet prepared to face the ontological implications of his existence, and felt assured that he was wrestling with the same reservations.

I wrote on many of the house's other windows, carrying a kettle of boiling water room to room to fog the glass. I left personalized hellos to June, my mother, and Mr. Stick, along with generic hellos to any other ghost who might discover them, but only my bedroom window retained its foggy words and none of the other windows ever showed an answer.

Sometimes I woke with no recollection of falling asleep—

only a vague remembrance of insomnia—and felt the cosmic gap that yawned between days. Long ago, I didn't exist. Would I cease to be again? What if the voids before and after, and the night-gulfs between, were truer than the twinkling lights that constituted life?

I had nightmares of waking up to solitude again.

One night as I was preparing for bed, I switched off my radio and the music kept playing at the lowest perceptible volume. A lingering charge in the radio, I thought, or a tuning-fork effect in my inner ear's bones. And yet the music carried on, delicate and ghostly. I had to hold my breath to hear the melody unfurl.

It was Mr. Gormly's radio playing in the basement. I was two floors above him but his music floated up, maybe through the radiator pipes or hidden ducts.

I hurried down from my bedroom, determined to finally meet him. But although I made little sound in my descent, he must have heard me coming because the music stopped playing. When I opened the basement door, the stairs were unlit and I regretted leaving my pocketlight behind.

"Hello?" I said in the dark. "Mr. Gormly, this is William. I've been hoping we could talk."

Not a word, not a rustle followed my appeal. I used the railing to feel my way down and pulled the lightbulb cord, which was inconveniently placed at the bottom of the stairs.

The cord, no longer attached to the light fixture, tipped a bucketful of small, scrabbling insects into my hair. I shrieked and clambered back upstairs, swatting at my head and slamming the door behind me. The insects clung despite my frantic tousles, and as I fled to the bathroom for adequate light and a mirror, Mr. Gormly's radio resumed playing music.

I spent the next hour shampooing, combing, and tweezering my scalp.

Removal proved difficult as the insects rolled themselves tightly into my hair. My head was a thicket of writhing cocoons, and I began to seriously consider shaving my head when I finally managed to extract one for study.

I consulted Philo's *Enchiridion of Extraordinary Insects* and identified the vermin as Hungarian curlers. They were translucent gray, like blisters full of slush, with tacky abdomens that made them inextricable once they fully twisted into a host organism's hair.

After learning that common smoke irritated their membranes, I lit a tightly rolled newspaper, blew it out, and wafted the plume toward my head. The curlers began to uncoil themselves and tumble onto the floor, where I crushed them under my shoe heel. The sound was like bubble wrap popping underwater.

I took no pleasure in their extermination but they couldn't be allowed to further infest my home.

A single curler defied the smoke and I was forced to shave a portion of my hair with a straight razor. It left me with a bald patch, the size of a large postage stamp, to the left of my cowlick.

I admired this lone survivor's tenacity to live and kept the hair cocoon in a Mason jar, which I placed next to the jar of luminous snow water in the curiosities closet.

According to Philo, metamorphosis would take anywhere from one to seven months. Damage to the subsequent page prevented me from learning about its future winged form, but my anticipation was a hopeful end to a hideous ordeal.

After mopping the crushed Hungarian curlers off the floor, I decided to contact a lawyer about Addendum 7c of the

Affidavit of Title. I thought the incident might allow me to evict Mr. Gormly, and yet a deeper part of me wanted him to stay and negotiate his tenancy. I had the satisfying blood-rush of someone with an enemy and wanted to compel him to engage face to face.

June remained mercurial and oftentimes aloof.

Whenever I sensed she was near, I talked in the seemingly empty room and somehow, despite her lack of ears, she registered the soundwaves moving through the air. She saw me, too, and seemed to grow adept at interpreting my postures and expressions, whereas I never perceived so much as a vaporous silhouette of her form.

Her unpredictable comings and goings kept me off-guard. Every time I undressed, slept, talked to myself, or blew my nose, I knew she might silently appear without my noticing. My lack of privacy led to openness. As my physical exposure grew more and more familiar, I became more comfortable telling her about my life, just as being naked in the house had made me feel at home.

I told her about the things I'd experienced since moving in: the three-winged pigeon, Other William, my nightmare about an indescribable cat. I told her about my mother's trauma and my father's fatal crash. One night I sobbed in her presence, lonely and unmoored, unaware that she was there until I suddenly sensed her leaving.

She came and went without reason, appearing when I didn't expect her and disappearing—to where, and how?—as soon as I believed the two of us were bonding. I worried that my neediness would frighten her away and worried that my false nonchalance would do the same, and so I began to refrain from summoning her by writing on the window, and when she visited my room, I never asked where she'd been or why she'd come back.

I was essentially blind and deaf whenever we conversed, able to speak, emote, and gesture in fully-fleshed monologues while June remained invisible and mute. I couldn't decide which of us had it worse with my voice never answered and her answers never voiced.

Our only means of communication remained my bedroom's foggy window. She couldn't move objects, let alone grasp a pen, but somehow her fingertip could slowly streak the glass. Her energy—maybe a fundamental electrical charge she'd retained after death—had just enough force to move molecules of water.

But even that required extraordinary effort on her part and I devised a simpler method by drawing two columns on the window—Y and N, divided by a line—and asking her yes-or-no questions. All she had to do was dot the appropriate column.

She was taciturn and sometimes stubbornly withdrawn, but I phrased my questions carefully and slowly came to know certain details about her.

She was twenty-one years old, and yet I suspected death had made her something of an old soul.

She could be warm and even playful, as willing to share the room in silence as to tease me with enigmas. One night, she spent ten minutes drawing what I believed to be an occult symbol on the window. At the height of my suspense, she squeaked the first X in a game of tic-tac-toe.

She was sorrowful and scared and wouldn't tell why.

I knew nothing significant about her life before her death. She declined to answer questions on the subject and withdrew if I pressed too far, however subtle my attempt. Now and then I felt resentful, needing better than she offered. Other times, I blamed myself for needing more than giving.

One night I asked if she'd encountered other spirits, hoping she'd caught a glimpse of my mother, Mr. Stick, or anyone who had haunted the house long enough to know its secrets.

"No," June answered.

"Maybe you have and didn't realize. Do you ever feel as if you're not alone?"

"No."

"Have you experienced any subtle changes of atmosphere you can't explain?"

"No."

"How about a change you can explain?"

"No."

"Have you seen anything remarkable I haven't already mentioned?"

"No."

We both grew impatient with our mode of conversation. Every small exchange was a game of twenty questions, riddled with mysterious abstractions and confusion.

I plunged into reading, hoping to learn more about the physics and abilities of disembodied spirits, of which there seem to be as many varieties as common living people, and we began to experiment with alternate means of communication.

She couldn't move a Ouija board planchette. She was unable to write in a layer of superfine ash, which I had delicately poofed across a white lacquered table. I attempted a spell on myself called the Katten Oren, which briefly allowed me to hear every mouse and insect scuttling in my brownstone but not a trace of June's voice or any of her movements.

Late one night, after a grueling day of study, I was sitting with June at the end of the bed, exhausted from my work and lapsing into sleep. My hand fell open. June twirled her finger in the center of my palm. I smiled, half-sleeping, at the feeling of her touch, which was not exactly physical and not exactly psychic. It was more as if the spirit in my hand was made of water and the spirit in her fingertip had delicately swirled it.

I jolted up and faced her, staring mid-distance at the spot I thought her face would be.

"Tell me if you just drew a circle. Y or N."

I held my upturned palm toward her on the bed. She wrote a thick "Y", clear and perfect, in my hand.

"What color are the walls?" I asked.

She wrote the word, "BROWN."

I laughed and spun, dizzy from the inside out, and thought I felt her staring very hard in my direction. Then her presence seemed to flicker and I worried she had vanished.

"Are you here?" I asked.

She wrote the word "YES" inside my palm.

"We did it! We can talk now!"

June didn't answer. I wondered if the breakthrough had frightened her somehow and thought about a thing my mother once said—that ghosts were only people, after all, same as me, and were as hesitant to show themselves as anybody else.

"June," I said.

Nothing.

"Please don't disappear again. Tell me about yourself. Why are you here?"

"I DON'T KNOW."

"Is there anything you need?"

She wrote the word, "DEATH," in the middle of my forehead.

4. ALONE TOGETHER

Communicating by psychokinetic touch took some getting used to.

June's ease in tracing letters on my skin contrasted with my struggle to identify the shapes. Depending on her position in relation to my hand, her letters would appear in various directions. Sitting beside me, they were normal, but whenever she stood in front of me, her letters were backwards and upside-down on my upturned palm.

I asked her to use only capital letters, eleven of which are vertically symmetrical, and my mind soon adapted to the remainder's backward shapes. Upside-down was harder. But the greater challenge was piecing together words, and ultimately sentences, from a series of overlapping, rapid-fire letters. Whenever I lost the thread, every letter thereafter tumbled into chaos, and June was often forced to clarify or repeat her thoughts completely.

But immersion worked wonders and we quickly grew fluent. I continued to speak aloud, knowing she could hear me, and although we'd been communicating on the foggy glass for weeks, our freedom from yes-or-no exchanges felt revelatory and new.

"THANKS," June said.

"For what?"

"FIGURING THIS OUT."

"Thanks for talking to me. You've been my only friend since

I moved here. Actually, you've been my only friend in a long time."

I smiled when I said it, wondering if smiles could exist without bodies. I decided they could and felt—or hoped—June was smiling back.

"LONER CLUB," she said. "NEVER REALLY TOGETHER."

"Of course we are. It's like a phone conversation."

"TEXTING FROM BEYOND."

"We're a long-distance relationship in the same room."

"LIKE EVERY RELATIONSHIP. SORRY."

"For what?"

"PESSIMISTIC BEING DEAD."

I had already asked her twice why she'd written the word "death" when I'd asked her what she needed. She claimed she'd written "breath" because she'd wanted a pause to calm herself, excited as she'd been to properly communicate. I sensed it wasn't true but didn't want to push.

"Tell me everything," I said. "What's your last name?"

"ASK SOMETHING ELSE."

I had exposed myself for weeks, physically and emotionally. That she wouldn't share her name seemed grossly unfair. Was she hiding her identity or harboring a secret? Instead of showing my frustration, I took a long pause and listened to my nightstand clock, which I'd partly learned to interpret by the rhythm of its ticks. It was after 3 a.m., a time when the clock seemed reluctant to advance.

"Did you live nearby?" I asked.

"YES," June said.

"Is your family here, too?"

"NO."

"We're beyond yes and no," I said. "I want to get to know you. It hurts me that we're finally able to talk and you're refusing."

"I'M SORRY."

"Tell me anything you can."

"I DON'T REMEMBER."

"You don't remember what?"

"MY LIFE," June said.

Recalling our window conversations from the previous weeks, I realized how little I'd actually learned about her, and how much of her vagueness I'd attributed to the limits of our yes-or-no talks.

"You don't have a brain!" I said, excited by a theory I had frequently considered. "If your memories existed in your synapses and neurons, it only makes sense that most of them were lost."

She radiated grief, like a dark solar wind, and left me feeling poisoned.

"June," I said. "I'm sorry. It's just an idea that probably isn't true."

Her energy subsided to a low-grade heat. When I felt she was calmer, I extended my open palm and said, "You know your name and how to write. The rest of it will come."

"MY LIFE IS ALWAYS SOMEWHERE ELSE."

"I don't understand."

"IT'S LIKE THE WHOLE ME, THE PERFECT ME, IS TOTALLY OUT OF REACH. I FEEL IT BUT I'M TRAPPED HERE. THERE'S NOTHING I CAN DO."

My room seemed to shrink. The brick walls surrounded us, the pressed-tin ceiling sagged overhead, and the dark closed around us like a black rubber bag. We sat together on the bed without quite touching and a gentle, rippling static—did I imagine it?—connected us.

"Where do you go when you're not here?" I asked.

"I DON'T KNOW. BUT IT'S FAMILIAR. LIKE A PLACE I'VE KNOWN FOREVER."

"Is it a choice or are you pulled there?"

"BOTH," she said. "NEITHER."

"Can you describe it? How does it feel?"

The bond between us waned. I felt a hollowness inside me that I remembered from my mother when I'd sensed, without my body, that she had left me all alone. I concentrated on June and knew, with an instinct that felt like extrasensory perception, the position of her limbs as her form sat beside me. I touched her on the arm—invisible air, faint with Juneness—and her presence coalesced and richened in my hand.

"You're here with me tonight," I said. "I'll help however I can."

We stretched back in bed, side by side, staring up. The ceiling's star designs, mysterious and subtle from the streetlight's glow, were strange constellations in the dark, decrepit tin. My thoughts descended, thick and heavy from a deeper sort of gravity, and nothing felt real expect the two of us together. I listened to my clock, wishing it would stick, and felt my consciousness of everything begin to disappear.

She was gone the next morning, and while her absence didn't surprise me, the thought of her alone wrenched me more than usual, and the memory of her fingertip writing on my hand gave my own solitude an extra palpability. I stayed in bed a while longer as the radiators' twisted pipes sang their ghastly chorus and the midwinter sun, hindered by the clouds, made a halfhearted effort to illuminate the room. But my renewed avidity to study June's condition—the condition of anyone capable of communicating after death—overcame my leadenness.

I dressed, brushed my teeth, and went downstairs for breakfast.

Prior to that morning, I had never stood in my kitchen at precisely 8:33 a.m. Normally, I woke much earlier, ate my cinnamon banana, and carried a fresh carafe of coffee from the kitchen to the study. On that day, though, I turned with the full carafe and saw a middle-aged woman leaning against the sink.

I spasmed in surprise, sloshing coffee onto the wall and overturning the mortar and pestle I'd used for my banana.

The woman noticed none of this and calmly smoked a cigarette. She stood barefoot in a nightgown, wearing cat's eye glasses and curlers in her hair. She held a three-inch paring knife softly at her hip.

Then a man entered the kitchen, surprising me anew, and stood in a blank spot of the room as if a table were before him. He wore a suit and tie, along with a fedora, and placed his briefcase on the floor without acknowledging the woman. He appeared to eat something, perhaps a phantom donut, from the invisible table.

The couple moved like a silent film projected onto mist. I suspected I was witnessing an old, hostile marriage—a scene from fifty years ago, repeated so many times, and with so little variation, that the couple's habitual morning had been burned, like a living memory, into the kitchen's atmosphere.

The husband turned to his wife. He made a fist, unbuttoned one of his cuffs, and pushed his sleeve halfway up his arm. The wife met his eye and dropped her cigarette into the sink.

She held her husband's hand, raised the paring knife, and drew the blade straight across the muscle of his forearm. The cut was short and neat but deep enough to bleed.

She offered him the knife. He cut her arm identically.

They applied bandages to each other's wounds. The wife rinsed the blade while her husband refastened his cuff, and then without a word or a kiss goodbye, she lit another cigarette and watched him leave for work. As soon as he was gone, she vanished from the room.

I paper-toweled my spilled coffee off the floor and wall, started another pot, and pondered what I'd witnessed. My earliest impression of the couple had been wrong. Their ritual of harm and care, far from being hostile, bore the bold peculiarity of genuine devotion. The specifics of their bloodletting seemed to matter less than that they'd marked each other often, secretly and strangely.

Remarkable as the kitchen encounter had been, I hurried up to my study with caffeinated fervor, determined to read, think, and intuit my way to a deeper understanding of June's limbo and how I might continue to bridge the gap between us. More immediately pressing was the three-winged pigeon. I had slept so late, I was in danger of missing his 9 a.m. visit and barely had time to prep for his arrival.

The previous morning had been unusually warm for winter, and I had opened the window and rested my coffee mug on the sill. The pigeon had perched beside it with his head wreathed in steam and looked from me to the mug with marvelous intensity. As usual, he'd displayed no interest in the food I had left him, but his fixation with the steaming mug had given me an idea.

Today I opened the sash and filled his bowl with coffee beans. They were dark-roast beans, oily black and aromatic, and I kept a handful to chew while I sat in my reading chair and waited for the pigeon to arrive.

He landed on time, folded his wings, and cocked his head at me. I'd left the window open, giving him ample room to move around the sill, and after warming himself for a minute, he bobbed toward the food bowl and eyed it with suspicion. He stared a long time and puffed out his chest, and then he finally took a bean and cracked it with his beak.

Before I could smile, I felt an exclamation point written on my hand and jerked out of my seat, swatting at the air. The pigeon exploded into flight and corkscrewed away.

"June?" I said.

"BOO. YOU'RE RIDICULOUSLY JUMPY FOR A GHOST ENTHUSIAST."

"I didn't expect you back this soon."

"I DIDN'T LEAVE. I GOT BORED WATCHING YOU SLEEP AND WALKED AROUND THE HOUSE. SORRY I MADE YOU SCARE THE PIGEON. WHAT DID HE FINALLY LIKE?"

"Coffee beans."

"NEAT," she said. "P.S. ABOUT THE HOUSE. CAN YOU OPEN MORE DOORS? I CAN'T EXPLORE WHEN EVERYTHING'S SHUT."

"I didn't know you ever left the bedroom."

"SERIOUSLY?"

"I guess I just assumed. It's always where you are."

"IT'S WHERE YOU NOTICE ME," she said. "NOT COUNTING THE DAY YOU LOCKED ME IN THE CLOSET."

I flumped into the chair and opened my palm along the armrest. "I'm so sorry about that. If I'd had any idea—"

"FORGET IT, IT'S OK. THERE'S WORSE THINGS THAN GETTING TRAPPED IN A TINY DARK SPACE

BY YOUR ONLY FRIEND. LIKE GETTING VERRRY SLOWLY SUFFOCATED BY YOUR ONLY FRIEND."

"You weren't actually killed by your only friend, were you?"

"I DON'T REMEMBER HAVING FRIENDS. I WONDER WHY. I'M SUCH AN UPPER."

"You are to me."

"BECAUSE YOU'RE LONELY AND YOU DON'T KNOW A THING ABOUT ME. MY BEST TRAITS ARE BEING QUIET AND INVISIBLE."

"Have I really not noticed you a lot? I can't believe I locked you in and never had a clue. But if you're able to appear and disappear sometimes, why'd you stay in the closet?"

"YOU'RE OBSESSED WITH THE CLOSET."

"I want to figure out the laws of your existence."

"THAT'S A REALLY GOOD LINE. NO WONDER I GO TO YOUR BEDROOM. SO FINE, I'LL TRY TO EXPLAIN IT. I DON'T DISAPPEAR AND REAPPEAR THE WAY YOU THINK. WHEN I FADE, IT'S LIKE A COMA. LIKE I'M CEASING TO EXIST. IT'S NOTHING WHEN I'M IN IT BUT IT'S TERRIFYING GOING THERE."

"How do you come back?"

"I SEE YOU LIKE A DREAM. LIKE A PERSON I'VE IMAGINED. EVENTUALLY, IF I'M LUCKY, THE HOUSE APPEARS, TOO."

"Is it easier to do now that we're connecting more?"

"IT'S QUICKER NOW," she said. "BUT I'M NEVER IN CONTROL."

"And you've appeared without me noticing?"

"I'M WITH YOU HERE IN THE STUDY A LOT. I SIT AND WATCH YOU READ."

I thought of all the times I must have picked my nose, adjusted my crotch, and talked to myself when she was secretly beside me.

"You just sit here and watch?"

"I SORT OF MEDITATE OR DAYDREAM WITHOUT REALLY THINKING. I GUESS IT'S HOW I SLEEP."

"Why don't you let me know you're here?"

"I LIKE YOUR COMPANY," she said, "BUT SOMETIMES I'D RATHER JUST LURK THAN INTERACT. I'LL STOP IF IT FREAKS YOU OUT."

"It does a little. But don't stop. It's fine if you don't want to talk, but maybe let me know you're sitting in the room."

"I FEEL LIKE A CREEPY VOYEUR NOW."

"It's nice you want to be with me."

"WHY?"

"What do you mean?"

"YOU DON'T SEEM TO LIKE COMPANY. YOU NEVER CALL ANYONE OR LEAVE THE HOUSE."

"I've already met you. Talking to you is important to me."

"WOULDN'T YOU RATHER MEET SOMEBODY ALIVE?"

"You're alive," I said. "And connections like this don't happen very often, at least not for me. When they do, I make the most of them before they disappear."

"IT'S HAPPENED TO YOU BEFORE."

"You know about my parents."

"BUT THERE WERE OTHER PEOPLE, TOO," she said. "TELL ME ABOUT A GIRL YOU LOST. AND NOT JUST AN ORDINARY BREAKUP STORY. TELL ME ONE THAT REALLY MADE YOU SCARED OF

PEOPLE VANISHING."

Her request was so incisive, she almost seemed psychic, and I didn't have to think of which story I would tell her.

"Her name was Nique," I said. "Like Monique or Veronique."

"WHICH WAS IT?"

"Her name was just Nique. We were both fourteen. The high school was new to me and I wasn't making friends. I'd switched out of my previous school because I'd gotten a reputation for being weird."

"YOU?"

"Let's just say I'd learned not to read witchcraft and necromancy books in study hall. In the new school, I left my books home and kept a lower profile. I sat alone at lunch, sketching ghosts and occult symbols in a notebook.

"Nique was a loner, too. I never knew why. She was confident, smart, cute. But she always beelined away from classmates, and even I didn't notice her until this one day in the cafeteria when she walked up behind me and saw me drawing a demon. I was embarrassed and closed the notebook, but then she sat across the table and asked me if I ever drew people. I didn't—not ordinary people, anyway—but I lied and said yes. She told me to draw her.

"I don't remember how I answered but I opened my notebook and gave it a shot. Some kids from other tables were looking in our direction, and I kept thinking it had to be a trick that she was talking to me at all. My hands were shaking when I started, and she just sat there and watched me while I tried to draw her as artfully as possible.

"Her stare was so persistent, I forgot the other kids who were watching us and did an OK job. Her ears were right. Her nose was two-dimensional and smudged. Her eyes were good, placed a little higher than they should have been but pretty well shaped and properly intense. I spun the notebook to show her.

"She said it was terrible but that I could try more at home and show her tomorrow. I tried drawing her from memory that night. The next day she came back to my table and I showed her the new picture. 'Draw me how I am,' she said. 'Not the way I look.' I didn't understand what she wanted me to do, but then she said, 'Get it right, and I'll let you kiss me.' I couldn't tell if she was teasing me, but I'd never kissed anyone before and I took her offer seriously. I thought kissing Nique would turn things around for me. I wouldn't suddenly be popular. I didn't really *want* that. But the idea of having a weird girlfriend—somebody like me—was irresistible.

"I drew her face every night and tried to get it right. I showed her my best attempts and every time she said, 'Nope,' but she came to my table at the start of every lunch and stayed until the end. We talked about school and music, classmates we liked and didn't like. She had four older siblings, owned six hundred comic books, and did embroideries of women with plants growing out of their bodies. She wrote a secret blog but wouldn't tell me how to find it. We had a conversation one day I remember almost verbatim.

"Why'd you start talking to me? I asked.

"Why not? she said.

"You don't talk to anybody else.

"Maybe you're a mystery.

"What if you think I'm boring once you figure me out?

"Good mysteries don't work that way, she said.

"How do they work?

"They never end. She fluttered her hands in front of her face like an amateur magician. *I'll show you a trick. Close your eyes. I'll*

disappear and reappear.

"I closed my eyes and heard her chair scrape away from the table, and I had this terrible feeling that she'd walked away, and that everybody in the cafeteria was watching me sit there alone with my eyes closed. So I looked and there she was, exactly as she'd been, only prettier than before and more immediate somehow.

"She looked at me and smiled and said the word, *Poof!*

"I didn't know if we were a couple and I still hadn't kissed her. I started drawing her different ways at night but didn't show her my attempts for a week or two. I drew her as a supervillain. Drew her as a bird. Drew her reading, running, sleeping. Drew her ghostly. Drew her naked. I was obsessed with the hidden parts of her life, the stuff she hadn't told me and the things I hadn't asked.

"Two days before Christmas, on the last morning of school before the winter break, I followed her into the school library, where nobody but Nique ever went unless they needed to. I found her in a cubby with a Japanese comic, reading it back to front. I was feeling clever and told her I'd finally gotten her picture right, and then I held a sheet of tracing paper up between our faces. I saw her as a blur. She leaned in close and kissed me through the sheet. Our mouths and noses crinkled together, and then she folded the paper into her comic and walked with me to class.

"Our lunch together felt both easier and harder. Normal in another way, like everything had changed without really changing. I wasn't even sure that had counted as a kiss but it was our first kiss, and I remember wishing Nique had let me keep the tracing paper.

"We were out of school for ten days. Nique was traveling

with her family, staying with relatives for the holidays. She didn't have a cellphone yet. She'd been certain her parents had bought her one for Christmas, and she promised me she'd call as soon as she had a number.

"Christmas came and went. I didn't know her relatives' number, so I emailed her the next day, and every day after that, but she didn't write back. Maybe she hadn't gotten a cellphone, and maybe she hadn't checked email, but her relatives had a phone and Nique wasn't calling. I wondered if her parents wouldn't let her call, but if the roles had been reversed, I'd have found a way to reach her. I worried she was sick, or that her family had gotten into an accident and she was in a hospital somewhere. I emailed and emailed. I didn't know what to do.

"I spent the whole break waiting for classes to start again. The morning of the first day back, I woke up early, afraid I'd walk into school and find out something terrible had happened. I imagined all the students being led into the auditorium so the principal could tell us Nique had tragically died.

"Instead I walked into homeroom and saw her in the back. She was talking with two classmates she'd never shown interest in talking to before. She had a cellphone in her hand. I went up to her and said *hey*. The three of them looked at me, and my face felt hot and twitchy and ridiculous. She said *hey* back and it was casual and flat.

"I asked if we could talk and she looked embarrassed, walking across the room so we could stand in the corner. I swarmed her with questions. *How long had she been back in town? Why hadn't she called or emailed? Was everything OK? What was going on?*

"She gave me vague, shruggy answers—her phone was acting weird, she'd been busy with her family, everything was fine and nothing was going on. She made it seem as if my questions were peculiar and excessive, like I didn't really know her well enough to ask. She gave me nowhere to go and nothing else to say. I was so confused and hurt I just went to my desk, and she went back to hers, and we sat through our classes without another word.

"I sat alone at lunch. She sat with the classmates she'd been talking to in homeroom. I couldn't catch her eye, and I was too humiliated to interrupt her group again, especially in front of the entire lunchroom. And that was it. She'd gone on winter break and simply moved on. I never knew if I'd done something wrong, or if she'd always been cruel, or if she'd somehow changed that deeply in a week."

June sat without answering after I was done. For a while I was quiet in the wake of what I'd told her, swirling in the details my memory had raised. Cafeteria milk from house-shaped cartons. The feel of tracing paper crinkling into the shape of pressed lips. All the drawings I had done, most of which I vividly remembered even though I struggled to recall Nique's face.

"THAT SUCKS," June said. "DID YOU HATE HER AFTER THAT?"

"I was bitter but I missed her."

"DID YOU MISS HER SPECIFICALLY, OR DID YOU ONLY MISS THE FACT THAT ANYONE HAD TALKED TO YOU?"

"After drawing her, and thinking of her, and talking to her for weeks, I'd been positive I knew her. I really missed *her*."

"DID YOU WONDER HOW MUCH OF HER YOU MIGHT HAVE JUST INVENTED?"

"I liked the parts of her I knew."

"BUT WHAT IF SHE WAS SHOWING YOU A VERSION OF HERSELF AND YOU WERE CRUSHING ON THAT INSTEAD OF SOMEONE REAL?"

"Why are you asking this?" I said, as if my memory were threatened.

"WOULDN'T THAT HAVE HURT?"

"Of course it would have hurt. But what am I supposed to do? Spend my life doubting everyone I meet?"

"FORGET IT," June said. "I'M SORRY YOU LOST YOUR FRIEND."

I didn't feel like talking anymore and neither did she. One of my candles had guttered and the wick had smoked longer than a wick normally smoked. The coils in the air seemed purposefully designed and had a fragrance that reminded me of childhood birthdays. Candles on a cake. Sickly sweet frosting. Gifts seeming duller after they were opened. The room felt dense and energy-deprived, as if the memory I'd shared had sugar-crashed the day.

I suggested leaving the study and touring the house.

"I'll open more doors so you can explore whenever you want."

"SHOULDN'T YOU BE READING?"

"Is that what you want me to do?"

"HOW ELSE ARE YOU GOING TO FIGURE OUT THE LAWS OF MY EXISTENCE?"

My desk and floor were strewn with books as I deepened my knowledge of astral bodies, purgatorial planes, and hypotheses about the nature of memory and its persistence in the absence of a physical brain. If my kitchen retained the memory of a long-gone couple, maybe the space around June held her own scattered memories and all we needed to do was focus them with questions.

We talked on and off throughout the day, but mostly we

were quiet as she read over my shoulder, listened to music, and either daydreamed or watched me as she moved around the room. She was so unobtrusive—and I was so immersed in my books—that several times I stopped reading, discovered an hour had passed, and needed reassurance that she hadn't disappeared. I had nothing but coffee until dinner, and then we sat together in the kitchen, where I made myself a giant bowl of angel hair pasta and told her about the married couple I had witnessed that morning.

"I don't think they're real," I said.

"MAYBE I'M NOT, EITHER."

"I meant they're only afterglows of life."

"SO DID I."

"The couple is like a movie. With you, it's totally different."

"HOW?" June said.

"You talk to me. You improvise. There isn't any script."

I kept studying after dinner until my brain felt bloodshot. All I wanted was to talk with June to feel her and connect again. We walked together to my room, where she lay on the bed and waited while I went in the adjoining bathroom, closed the door, and showered. The pipes had been only partially distorted by the superheated water there, and their reliable pressure and warm, harmonic hum relieved the tension in my overworked intellect and shoulders.

I toweled off, dressed in boxers and an undershirt, and opened the door. June crossed the room and stood beside me at the sink. I noticed that the shower steam swirled as she approached. It was the first time I'd seen her affect the physical world aside from my body and the window fog, and as I started brushing my teeth, I realized all three—me, the fog, and the steam—shared the element of water.

"I MISS BRUSHING MY TEETH," she wrote on my free hand.

I spat the foam and rinsed. "Are your memories coming back?"

June didn't answer.

"Can I ask you more questions? If we focus on specific details, especially about your body, we might be able to spark connections to the physical life you had."

She paused and said, "OK."

I turned the lights out to reduce external stimuli and we laid together in bed, side by side and facing up, with my open palm between us and her finger tracing letters.

"You remember clean teeth," I said. "What else do you remember about your body?"

She didn't answer for a minute and her presence seemed to dim. I sensed she wasn't darkening but radiating inward, like a special bulb illuminating nothing but itself.

"ONE OF MY TEETH WAS CROOKED. IT WAS MY UPPER RIGHT LATERAL INCISOR. I USED TO PRACTICE HOW TO SMILE SO THE TOOTH WOULDN'T SHOW."

I'd done the same when I was younger, not to hide a crooked tooth but to smile more naturally, without self-awareness. I'd never grown familiar with the workings of my face.

"What else?" I asked.

"MY BOOBS WERE PRETTY GREAT. THEY WERE PERKY WITHOUT BEING OBNOXIOUS ABOUT IT. BUT MY HIPS AND THIGHS WERE TOO BIG. I KNOW EVERYBODY SAYS THAT BUT IT REALLY LOOKED LIKE A FACTORY MIXUP. LIKE A STURDIER GIRL WALKED AWAY WITH SKINNY

JUNE LEGS, AND ALL THEY HAD LEFT FOR ME WERE STURDY-GIRL LEGS."

"Were you short or tall?"

"MEDIUM."

"What about your hair?"

"I CHANGED THAT A LOT. THE COLORS AND THE CUTS. I USUALLY KEPT IT LONG."

"Any scars or tattoos?"

"I HAD A BIRTHMARK," she said. "A PORT-WINE STAIN. IT'S CALLED A FIREMARK, TOO. I LIKED THE SOUND OF THAT BETTER."

"Where was it?"

"ON MY BACK. IT RAN FROM THE TOP OF MY NECK TO JUST ABOVE MY WAIST. IT'S WHY I KEPT MY HAIR LONG AND NEVER WORE BIKINIS. I ALMOST STARTED TO LOVE IT RIGHT BEFORE I DIED."

"What shape was it?" I asked.

"HARD TO DESCRIBE. IT WAS ALWAYS JUST MY MARK. WHEN I THINK ABOUT IT NOW, IT SEEMS SIGNIFICANT SOMEHOW. LIKE A SYMBOL OR A CLUE I NEVER UNDERSTOOD."

I visualized her spine—she had her hair pulled aside and draped forward over a shoulder—with her birthmark moving like a dark tongue of fire, as soft as living skin underneath my hand.

"I DON'T KNOW WHERE I'M BURIED BUT I'M OUT THERE NOW. I'M FROZEN UNDERGROUND. IN THE SPRING, I'LL DECOMPOSE. MY EYES, MY GUTS, MY FIREMARK. EVERYTHING WILL ROT EXCEPT MY SKELETON AND HAIR."

I struggled to imagine the despondency she faced—an out-of-body experience that silently continued after the coroner, the mourners, and her flesh disappeared, leaving nothing but her lonely comprehension as a witness.

"Tell me about your eyes," I said.

"THEY WERE TOO FAR APART. I LIKED THAT THEY WERE BIG, BUT I HATED MAKING EYE CONTACT BECAUSE THEN PEOPLE WOULD EITHER IGNORE ME OR EXPECT SOMETHING ELSE."

"Which did you prefer?"

"NEITHER. I WAS A WEIRDO. I DIDN'T MAKE SENSE. I'D STARE AT MYSELF IN MIRRORS, PRETENDING THERE WERE TWO OF ME, FIGURING EACH OTHER OUT."

"Like me and Other William."

"HOW ARE YOU FEELING ABOUT THAT? DOESN'T IT FREAK YOU OUT THAT THERE'S A WHOLE SECOND YOU?"

"I'm getting used to the idea. It seems so familiar. I've heard myself talking to myself all my life, so it's really no stranger than it's always been."

"BUT THAT'S EXACTLY WHAT I MEAN. IT NEVER FELT RIGHT THAT I COULD BE MYSELF AND WATCH MYSELF LIKE TWO SEPARATE PEOPLE. WHEN I TALKED TO SOMEONE ELSE, I DIDN'T KNOW WHO I WAS, AND THEN I DIDN'T FEEL SEEN OR EVEN REALLY THERE."

"Do you feel that way with me?"

"USUALLY," she said. "NO OFFENSE. IT'S NOT YOUR FAULT. BEING DEAD HASN'T FIXED THE

PROBLEMS IN MY LIFE."

The bedroom's humidity had grown so marshy, condensation started dripping from the ceiling to the bed. One of the drops glinted briefly from the nearby streetlight and landed on my cheek.

"TAKE YOUR SHIRT OFF."

"Why?"

"I CAN'T TOUCH YOU THROUGH YOUR CLOTHES. RELAX. I WON'T POSSESS YOU."

I sat up in bed and tugged my undershirt off, and when I settled back down, June laid her hand flush across my chest. My solar plexus glowed. I closed my eyes and breathed. She moved her hand deeper into the space between my lungs until my heart was in her palm.

The radiators sang, then sputter-steamed quiet. I visualized her eyes, her hair, her firemark again. Somewhere in the world, there were photos of her face. Her voice was in a voicemail somebody had saved.

When her palm left my chest, it left a palpable impression like a handprint inside me.

"HOW DO YOU FEEL?" she asked.

"Possessed."

5. PHANTOM EVERYTHING

The morning sun was like an egg yolk spilling on the bed. I looked down and noticed I was sporting an erection, which was covered by my boxers and the sheet but still apparent.

"IT'S A GHOST," June said.

I sat and hid my lap completely with a pillow.

"GOD I MISS THAT."

"What?"

"FEELING THINGS," she said.

I wiped the day's cleansing tears out of my eyes to clear my thoughts. "How long have you been awake?"

"INVISIBLE SHRUG."

"You can't tell the difference?"

"I HAD THE MOST INCREDIBLY VIVID DREAM ABOUT KISSING A BOY IN A FOUNTAIN OF WARM CARAMEL. I TASTED IT. I FELT HIS TONGUE."

"You know when you've been dreaming, then."

"SOMETIMES," she said. "BUT NOW THAT I'M AWAKE, I HAVE THIS DESPERATE URGE TO PEE. I KNOW IT ISN'T REAL EXCEPT IT FEELS REALLY REAL."

"You have physical sensations?"

"I'M NEVER HUNGRY BUT I'D KILL FOR A SCOOP OF ICE CREAM. I'M NEVER COLD BUT I WANT TO COCOON MYSELF IN BLANKETS. I WANT

TO TOUCH MYSELF AND LIE IN THE SUN AND SIP HOT COFFEE. I HAVE CRAVINGS NONSTOP. IT'S PHANTOM LIMB TIMES EVERYTHING."

"If your cravings are psychosomatic, maybe you can imagine them away."

"OR SATISFY THEM ALL BY FANTASIZING BETTER. CAN I WATCH YOU EAT BREAKFAST?"

"The kitchen!" I said, twisting around to look at my clock. "Come on, we've got to hurry. The couple with the knife might appear in ten minutes."

Ignoring my own need to urinate, I flung aside the pillow and sheet, quickly dressed, and buttoned my shirt on the way downstairs with June close behind me. We reached the kitchen with time to spare, so I sliced a banana into my mortar, sprinkled in some cinnamon, and mashed it with the pestle.

"WHAT ARE YOU DOING?"

"Making breakfast."

"I'M NOT IMAGINING BEING HUNGRY ANYMORE. WHY ARE YOU EATING BABY FOOD?"

The scent of spiced banana softened something in me.

"I honestly don't know," I said. "I had a sudden need to eat this two winters ago. The taste was so familiar. It was like eating a memory of my mother. After a few weeks, the memory faded and it just started tasting like breakfast on my own. Maybe now that you're here, I'll associate cinnamon banana with you."

"I'D SAY THAT'S REALLY WEIRD EXCEPT IT'S REALLY WEIRDLY NORMAL. I KEEP REMEMBERING THE SEDIMENTY PART OF APPLE CIDER. IT TASTES LIKE BEING SAFE BUT I CAN'T REMEMBER WHY."

I was about to fill the coffee pot when the ghostly wife materialized at the sink. Her appearance and behavior were the same as on the previous morning. She stood in her nightgown, holding the knife and smoking her cigarette, and seemed indifferent when her husband walked in, put his briefcase down, and rolled up his sleeve. June and I watched their bloodletting ritual in silence, and even after they'd bandaged each other's cuts and vanished, neither of us spoke until the atmosphere had cleared.

"THAT'S PRETTY FUCKED UP. IT'S ALSO PRETTY GREAT," she said. "IMAGINE BEING SOMEONE EVEN ROOMS CAN'T FORGET."

After eating my banana and drinking two cups of coffee, I gave June a proper tour of the house, opening doors and exploring rooms she hadn't yet seen. The day was brightly cold, the house was dark and warm, and our companionship had the coziness of a midwinter fire. I showed her where various phenomena had happened—the flameless candlelight in the black room, the wallpaper that slowly peeled and reapplied itself in the third-floor hall, the sparkling miasma in the broken dumbwaiter—and even drab, familiar spaces felt new with June beside me.

We puttered around the oddments room, which a previous inhabitant had used as a repository for debris, mysterious tools, and antediluvian equipment. Lit by a 22-watt lightbulb—the only such bulb I had ever encountered—the room's cluttered assortment looked as if a group of Frankensteinian robots had destroyed one another in a berserk battle royale and left behind a treasure trove of items I could use.

Continuing our tour, I felt a strong compulsion to enter the large, empty room at the far end of the dining room. It was an unremarkable space I'd rarely visited or thought about. I shined my pocketlight inside and discovered a small tree growing sideways out of the eastern wall.

"That's new," I said to June.

The room was square but subtly distorted, becoming wider and taller away from the entrance, which made me feel that I was shrinking as we moved toward the tree. The floor was rough-hewn planks, the walls were brown brick, and the air smelled of worms and childhood mud.

We examined the three-foot sapling that had sprouted from the bricks. Its trunk was horizontal and its roots gripped the mortar. A minor flow of water dribbled from the ceiling—probably from one of my distorted pipes—and dampened the wall just enough to give the sapling moisture. Its leaves were baby-aspirin orange.

I turned to the window across the room and said, "I should open the shutters."

"DON'T," June said.

"There isn't any light."

She tapped my hand in such a way that I was hesitant to move, as if she wanted to draw attention to a thing I ought to see. One of the tree's twigs sinuously turned. Its leaves began to undulate and point in June's direction. I imagined she had raised one finger to the twig and that the twig had reached back. The two of them were touching. I raised my own finger but the tree didn't notice, and my arm sank down in disappointment, even jealousy.

"I USED TO HAVE A LEMON TREE IN MY BEDROOM," June said. "IT WAS SMALL AND GREW EXACTLY ONE LEMON AT A TIME."

"You remember having a lemon tree?"

"I STRUNG IT WITH LIGHTS IN WINTER AND GAVE IT A STAR FOR CHRISTMAS. I CLEANED ITS

LEAVES. I FERTILIZED AND PRUNED IT JUST RIGHT.
ONE SPRING I TOOK IT OUTSIDE, THINKING THE
LIGHT WOULD HELP IT, BUT THE SUN BURNT ITS
LEAVES. IT WAS DEAD A MONTH LATER."

"Do you remember anything else?"

"I BLAMED MYSELF. I CRIED."

"I mean about your life."

"IT'S SAFER IN THE DARK," she said.

I kept the shutters locked despite my reservations, and when
we walked out of the room, June insisted I close the door behind
us, concerned that even ambient light could jeopardize the tree.
We walked through the dining room and out to the hallway,
where I asked her which room she'd like to see next. She didn't
answer and I sensed her energy had changed.

"Are you all right?" I asked.

"YES."

"Did something bother you in there?"

"NO."

"We don't have to tour the rest of the house. We can do
whatever you want."

"I'M FINE," she said. "LET'S GO."

I trusted her, or rather played along instead of pressing, and
we walked down the sconce-lit hall to the rear staircase so I
could lead her up to other rooms she hadn't yet seen.

The basement door stood at the end of the hallway, opposite
the stairwell. I paused there and placed my hand firmly on the
knob. I'd already told June about the Hungarian curler attack
but hadn't filled her in about a phone call I'd made.

"My lawyer said the booby-trap isn't grounds for
renegotiating tenancy. He told me that because I entered my
tenant's space without prior notice, I made myself liable to

undisclosed penalties if Mr. Gormly opts to file a complaint."

I cocked my ear toward the door to hear if his radio was playing.

"You know," I said, "*you* could go downstairs without him noticing. You might be able to see him."

My face filled with prickly heat when June didn't answer.

"That'd be wrong, though. A Gormly move. I wouldn't really ask you."

When she still didn't respond, I turned and said her name, and then I retraced my steps, reaching out and trying to feel her, and I was halfway up the hall before she finally touched my hand.

"There you are," I said. "I thought you were right behind me."

I sensed she was crouching near the wall and knelt beside her. She pawed at both my wrists, trying futilely to hold me.

"Hey. What's the matter?"

"FREAKING OUT," she said. "SCARED."

Her finger on my skin was sputtery and charged, like a brittle old wire with an unstable current. I couldn't tell her to breathe or put her head between her knees, so all I could do was keep her close and try to talk her through.

"Tell me what you feel."

"DARK," she said. "FALLING."

"What's scaring you?" I asked. "Is it the basement? Something else?"

She drew a circle in my palm that tightened to a spiral.

"Talk to me," I said. "I'm here with you. You're safe."

The spiral looped and looped until it seemed to draw itself and I was mesmerized, thinking we were feeling it together, even after she had panicked into vanishing again.

I walked through the house again, trying to sense June's energy in case she'd reappeared elsewhere after vanishing from the hallway. Rooms we'd visited together felt deader than before. It was as if the rooms themselves noticed June's absence when I entered them alone.

Everything seemed consciously determined to remind me. Clocks had expressions. Chairs had the bodiless design of missing bodies. I read alone in my study, thinking often of the tree growing in the dark and oftener of June—where she'd gone, who she was.

Late in the afternoon, the cast of light shifted. I remembered such light from napping as a child, when I would wake to find the sun orange and depleted, and it would seem as if a nameless and essential thing had died.

But then I remembered it was the night of the month's new moon—already its shadowy force seemed to infiltrate the house—and I knew Mr. Gormly would emerge to pay his rent. I thought of how June had panicked near the basement, and I resented being barred from further exploration. I sat at my desk and wrote a letter:

Dear Mr. Gormly,

I want us to be friendly or at very least civil. Nevertheless, please be apprised of the following requirements regarding our cohabitation.

You are not to enter my private rooms without permission. All future rent must be handed to me in person.

I require occasional access to the basement. You will be given twenty-four hours' notice prior to my entry.

Traps or obstructions must be removed.

Insects are not to be bred or kept on the premises.

If additional privacy is required, I will arrange for the construction of walls and a door around your quarters.

The basement lacks a bathroom. With respect to sanitary concerns, where and how are you performing your necessaries?

Sincerely,
William Rook

He had left the previous month's rent in my study, and since I suspected he was a creature of habit, I placed the letter in an envelope, labeled with his name, in the middle of my desk where he was likely to discover it.

A perfect opportunity popped into focus. I hid a motion-triggered camera, undetectable in the shadows, in one of my densely packed bookcases. The camera's lens was trained on my desk, where Mr. Gormly would pause to read my letter. I kept a single lamp on, so there was just enough light to illuminate the scene, and then I left the study, ate a quick dinner, and went to bed early.

Too early, it seemed, because as soon as I closed my eyes, my thoughts jumped and chattered and I couldn't stop twitching. The quiet house unsettled me. I listened for the creaks of miniature steps, increasingly unsure about my surreptitious plan. Legally speaking, I was almost certainly justified in photographing a hostile tenant who was entering my rooms under the cover of night, but then I thought of telling June and felt cowardly and small.

I decided with a moral glow to turn the camera off.

When I left my bed and returned to the study, Mr. Gormly

had already left his mint-scented envelope on my desk.

The camera snapped several photographs of me before I took it from the bookcase and deactivated the sensor. I was a button-click away from seeing Mr. Gormly on the digital display.

"Delete or look?" I asked myself.

My moral glow dimmed. I checked the photos on the miniature screen, arrowing past the pictures of myself and hesitating then, savoring the pause, before I arrowed one further to the shots of Mr. Gormly.

There were none. He wasn't there. Either he'd noticed the camera and deleted the pictures of himself, or his diminutive size had allowed him to move beneath the motion sensor's range.

Doubly deflated by the lack of photos and my lack of self-control, I turned the camera off and walked to my desk, where I opened Mr. Gormly's envelope and shook its contents onto my blotter.

In addition to the crisp hundred-dollar bill, a picture fluttered out and landed upside-down. I flipped it over. It was a small glossy image—not a Polaroid, mind you, but a well-developed photograph—of me concealing the camera on the shelf an hour earlier.

Judging by the vantage point and angle of the photo, I determined he'd used his own camera from the doorway and was approximately two feet tall.

Enclosed with the money and photo was a handwritten answer to my letter:

Our current living arrangement will suffice.

Sincerely,
Mr. Gormly

I threw his note across the room. The paper's harmless flutter exacerbated my frustration, but although I considered storming downstairs and pressing the matter directly, his cunning had unnerved me and I thought it best to wait until I thought of some way to mollify our feud.

June reappeared in my bedroom the following morning, but my relief in having her back was dampened by her reticence. She was unable or unwilling to explain her disappearance, and as I peppered her with questions—why had she panicked, where had she gone?—her "I don't knows" started to crackle with the same frantic energy she'd had the day before. Afraid of triggering another anxiety attack, I let the matter drop, and since I was too embarrassed to tell her about Mr. Gormly and the camera, we started the day with mutual reserve.

Our usual comfort returned, however, after we watched the couple's bloodletting ritual in the kitchen, walked up to my study, and saw the three-winged pigeon eat a dozen coffee beans.

"HE'S GONNA BE WIRED," June said. "HE'LL WANT A CIGARETTE NEXT."

My own senses sharpened with caffeine, I went to my desk and opened a marble notebook I'd been filling with ideas, excited to have a partner and a purpose to the day.

"I want to clarify your connection to the physical world," I said. "Not how or why you're here—not yet—but what you're able to experience without a material body. We'll need to try a lot of sensory experiments."

"SOUNDS LIKE A FUN DAY AT THE SECRET GOVERNMENT FACILITY."

"More like a weird doctor's visit."

We started with a vision test, using a standard physician's eye chart I taped to the wall. I stood beside June and asked her to trace the letters into my hand, beginning with the largest on top and moving to bottom. She scored perfectly until she read the final line as:

"B E W A R E T H E B L O O D Y C H I L D."

I squinted at the eye chart's randomized letters and said with thrilled alarm, "It reads that way to you? You're absolutely sure?"

"SUCKER," June said.

After determining her vision was excellent within a range of half a yard, I learned that anything farther away blurred increasingly with distance. She perceived fuzzy details at one yard, general shapes at two, and nothing whatsoever at three. If we stood at opposite ends of my study, she lost sight of me completely.

Her hearing was similar and therefore peculiar: a kind of auditory myopia that deadened sounds at very short distances. I played a record and the song was perfectly clear when she was directly at the speaker. She heard the song muffled at one yard, could barely discern the melody at two, and heard nothing at three—precisely where she also lost sight of the turntable.

Her entire audiovisual realm, in other words, was three yards in every direction: an eighteen-foot diameter existence, outside of which her world was mystery and fog.

"Come stand with me," I said, starting a new record at a volume just loud enough for me to hear precisely. "We're going to back away together, three feet at a time."

I walked backwards to the first interval, corked my ears gently with my fingertips, and partly narrowed my eyes, trying to replicate her one-third diminishment of sense. We moved together to the second interval, where I pressed my fingers deeper into my ears and almost fully closed my eyes. The music became a dull rhythm and a melody heard primarily from memory. The stereo was a shadowy box, visible but heavily obscured by my eyelashes. We backed up to the third and final interval, nine feet away from the starting point, and I squeezed my eyes shut and jammed my ears completely.

I realized how essential closeness was to June. She wasn't deaf and blind as my experiment had made me, but any time I moved beyond the limit of her senses, she saw herself alone inside a small, private bubble. Even up close, touch was everything to her, like a vibrating wire carrying her signal.

"I haven't really grasped how hard this is for you."

She wrote on my chest.

"THANKS FOR SAYING THAT. BUT CLOSING YOUR EYES AND PLUGGING YOUR EARS ISN'T GONNA DO IT."

I focused on the lull when her words stopped coming. My voice sounded private with my ears still blocked, as if the whole conversation was occurring in my head. I used to feel that way when I was sitting with my mother, unsure if she was registering anything I said.

"Before my mom finally died, it was harder when her haze lifted just a little. We'd talk and it'd be normal, but she'd always drift away again. I started feeling sick whenever we connected, knowing she'd be gone as soon as I enjoyed it."

"WHY'D YOU COME HERE, THEN? WHY NOT LET HER GO?"

"Trying to connect was something I could do. However much it hurt, it gave me some control. I guess it's automatic now. It's what I've done for years. But I'm still afraid of losing any good contact. A lot of times, reaching feels better than connecting."

June gripped my hand as if she really had a hand. The charge was so strong, I unplugged my ears, looked around the room, and found myself surprised by how immediate it seemed.

"I DON'T REMEMBER SOMEONE TRYING THIS HARD TO UNDERSTAND ME."

"How am I doing so far?"

"BETTER THAN I REALIZED."

A three-yard sphere of sensory input was all we really needed. Throughout the subsequent days and between my experiments, June didn't disappear and I rarely left her side. We spent hours sitting on my study's rug, poring over texts to understand her limbo. She could read on her own if I opened a book on the floor, and when she gently swiped my hand, I knew to turn her page. She slept at night in my bed, we woke together at dawn, and I learned more about her from simple companionship than I did from any research, experiments, or questions.

Our interactions preoccupied me more than anything else. I was undoubtedly overlooking fresh phenomena throughout the house, which I had mostly ceased to explore. Familiar marvels, such as the pigeon and the kitchen couple, were remarkable mostly because June and I encountered them together. My mother didn't cross my mind for hours at a time.

Quiet hours of reading seemed as natural to June as sudden bursts of mischief. One moment she would signal for a page turn, and the next she'd stick her finger in my ear, start a game of hangman on my forearm, or trace obscene symbols on my hand.

She shared sporadic memories—she was an only child, her favorite season was fall—but seemed to purposefully withhold or shy away from details. She often played silent, nimble music on my skin. When I asked if she remembered playing piano, she ignored me and refused to interact for half an hour. Other times, she opened up with startling directness.

One morning, I discovered a dusty bottle of perfume on the upper shelf on my bedroom closet. The fragrance was a vivifying rosemary-mint. June suggested it might have belonged to the ghostly wife in the kitchen. I closed my eyes to visualize the woman in her nightgown, excited to have another sensory impression of a person I would never know but wished to know better.

I dropped the bottle in distraction and it shattered at my feet. Instantly the scent vapor-drenched the air.

"Come in the closet with me," I said to June.

I offered her my hand, which she held without holding, and we stood in the narrow darkness once I closed the door.

"Can you smell that?"

"NO."

"Concentrate," I said.

"TELL ME WHAT IT'S LIKE."

The spilled perfume was dizzying. My stomach and my brain swirled in opposite directions, and suddenly I pictured brightly wrapped presents and a multicolored tree that lit my mother's cheek.

"It smells like Christmas rain," I said. "Like candy canes and wreaths."

I tucked my chin and lowered my eyes, knowing June was shorter, and our noses felt close enough to generate static.

"I REMEMBER SOMETHING."

"What?"

"THERE WAS A BOY."

"Who?"

"I MET HIM AFTER A PARTY IN A COAT-CHECK ROOM."

"What party?"

"I DON'T REMEMBER. IT WAS ONE OF THOSE COUNTRY-CLUBBY PLACES THAT HAS LOTS OF OFFICE PARTIES FOR THE HOLIDAYS. HE MUST HAVE COME FROM ONE OF THE OTHER PARTIES. HE WAS LOOKING FOR A COAT. HIS GIRLFRIEND'S, I THINK.

"THERE WAS NOBODY AT THE COAT-CHECK DESK. WE HAD TO LOOK ALONE. THE SPACE WAS REALLY TIGHT AND WE WERE RUBBING UP AGAINST EACH OTHER. I WAS DRUNK, JUST A LITTLE, AND HE WAS, TOO. HE WAS ROLLING A WINT O GREEN LIFE SAVER AROUND IN HIS MOUTH. I HEARD IT CLICK HIS TEETH. I TOLD HIM HOW THEY SPARK WHEN YOU CHEW THEM IN THE DARK. HE SAID EVERYBODY KNOWS THAT. I TOLD HIM HE SHOULD DO IT AND HE DIDN'T SAY A THING.

"AND IT WAS NO BIG DEAL EXCEPT IT FLATTENED ME. IT KILLED ME. JUST THE FACT HE DIDN'T BOTHER ANSWERING AT ALL. SO I SQUEEZED IN FRONT OF HIM AND KISSED HIM, WHICH WAS SUPER NOT ME, AND EVEN THEN HE LOOKED BORED. HE BARELY LOOKED SURPRISED. I WAS JUST SOME GIRL ACTING FLIGHTY AT A PARTY. SO I TOLD HIM I WAS DYING. I SAID I HAD A BRAIN TUMOR."

"Did you?"

"NO, I LIED. I TOLD HIM IT COULD KILL ME ANY TIME. THAT HE'D JUST KISSED A DEAD GIRL AND HADN'T EVEN KNOWN. HE STAMMERED

AND APOLOGIZED AND LEFT WITHOUT HIS GIRLFRIEND'S COAT. IT BOTHERED HIM A LOT. I LIKED THE WAY IT FELT."

"Why are you telling me this?" I asked.

"A LOT OF TIMES, I DIDN'T FEEL ALIVE WHEN I WAS ALIVE."

"That made you feel alive?"

"IT MADE ME FEEL REAL."

6. CENTIPEDES AND SMOKE

The fact that June had remembered something so complete should have been cause for excitement, but she behaved as if the story she had told me wasn't special. Had it moved her so strongly that she wanted to forget, or was her memory more intact than she had led me to believe? Whatever the explanation, her mood had a strange, almost tactile charge, as if her surface had electrified to guard something deeper.

When she wouldn't talk more about her memories of life, we went to my study for another round of sensory experiments.

"How does it feel to touch things?" I asked.

"IT'S LIKE THE PRESSURE WHEN A COUPLE LITTLE MAGNETS ARE REVERSED. THERE'S A SUBTLE PUSH BACK. IT DOESN'T FEEL STRONG ENOUGH TO MATTER BUT IT DOES, BECAUSE I NEVER REALLY TOUCH A THING, ASIDE FROM TOUCHING YOU."

"You're able to write in window fog. I've seen you move steam. Have you ever moved anything else? Even a little?"

"I DON'T THINK SO."

"Maybe you have and it's been too minor to notice."

"GO TO THE CHAIR WITH ME," she said.

I followed across the study to my claw-footed reading chair, which had come with the house and was more than a century old. The seat back had once been crudely reupholstered and bore the Y-shaped stitching of an autopsy scar.

"WATCH CLOSELY," June said.

I squatted with my face only inches from the seat, looking for the slightest perturbation of the cushion.

"Are you sitting now?" I asked.

"I WAS JUMPING ON THE SEAT," she said a moment later.

"I didn't see single mote of dust bounce up."

We experimented more. I balanced a marble on the faintest possible incline, so precariously that I wasn't able to back away without triggering its roll. June couldn't move it. I poofed baby powder into the air and she couldn't shift a speck. I gently draped a sheet between two chairs and was about to ask June to trampoline on it when she drifted up beside me and wrote on my cheek.

"HUG ME."

"That's an interesting idea," I said. "You can pass through my skin but never through my clothes. If I hold you wearing sleeves, with enough surrounding pressure, we might be able to overcome whatever repelling force prevents you from actual contact."

"I'M MELODRAMATICALLY SIGHING IN YOUR FACE. CAN YOU FEEL IT?"

"What's the matter?"

"QUIT THE SCIENCE FAIR AND HUG ME."

I ruffled with embarrassment and rolled down my sleeves.

"I'LL STAND IN FRONT OF YOU, OK?" she said. "HUG ME SO HARD, I CAN'T GET AWAY."

I ringed my arms in front of my body, grasped my own wrist, and gradually slid my hand up my arm to shrink the circle. My thumb reached my elbow and moved toward my armpit. I closed my eyes and concentrated, trying to feel the slightest change of pressure through my sleeves and wondering why I'd never tried clutching her before. When I realized my forearms were flat across my chest, I opened my eyes and felt around.

"June?"

"THAT WAS WEIRD."

I sighed and said, "Thank God. I thought I'd hugged you into halves."

"WHEN YOUR GRIP GOT TIGHT, I SQUISHED DOWN AND OUT. LIKE ONE OF THOSE WATER SNAKE TOYS THAT'S IMPOSSIBLE TO HOLD."

"What did it feel like?" I asked.

An amazing rill of heat ran along my jaw. My tongue laid softer in the bottom of my mouth.

"What was that?"

"I LICKED YOUR NECK. TAKE YOUR SHIRT OFF," she said.

I did as I was told with somnolent obedience, unable to sense her mood or name my own emotion. Even without my shirt, I couldn't really hold her, so I closed my eyes and let my arms dangle at my sides.

We stood together, leaning in, and let ourselves blend. She was shorter and I hunched until her face pressed my own, and then our features intermingled and her head was in my head. Her shoulders fit my shoulders and her chest filled my chest. She warmed me like a gin buzz, balsamy and floral, and my body felt smooth and marvelously fluid.

"Water!" I said and backed away. "You interact with fog and steam and the water in my body."

She paused, then wrote a question mark.

"What if I fill the bathtub and let you splash around? At

very least, I bet you'll make ripples on the surface."

"I DON'T WANT TO," she said.

"Let's try this. It'll be fun. You can cannonball and bellyflop and swan dive in. You can hold yourself under and you won't need to breathe."

June slashed a line across the middle of my face. It glowed like a razor cut just before it bleeds.

"What was that for?"

"I TOLD YOU NO. I'M SICK OF THESE EXPERIMENTS."

My thoughts were like a spiral gear moving in my head, turning nonstop but locked into place.

"You want me to figure things out, then suddenly you don't. I never know if you want me to ask questions, keep quiet, give you space, or come closer. You're impossible to read. What do you really want?"

"WHAT DO YOU WANT?" she said.

"This. You and me. Why would I want something else?"

"ME IN LIMBO MIGHT BE GREAT FOR YOU. IT'S TERRIBLE FOR ME."

"I'm doing everything I can for you. Somehow your spirit stayed connected to the world. Once we understand how—"

"I'LL STILL BE DEAD," June said.

A deep autumn hue pooled in around me like memories of things I wanted to forget.

"I know I haven't helped much. I'm reaching in the dark. But solutions won't come until we clarify the problems. It's frustrating now but we can solve this together."

I kept my hand extended but she didn't write more.

"June?" I said.

Nothing.

She might have disappeared or simply left the room, but either way she was gone, my body felt limp, and I was powerless to reach her if she didn't reach back.

I walked around the house, trying fruitlessly to find her, until I subconsciously brought myself to the third floor's unoccupied bedroom, sensing that my doppelgänger had done the same in his parallel brownstone.

I approached the roughhewn door, took a breath, and pulled the iron ring.

Other William did, too.

We looked at each other and sat in our respective wooden chairs, and although our rooms were feebly lit, my lifelong knowledge of my own physiognomy allowed me—and him, I assumed—to read each other's expressions with precision.

"It's good to see you again."

"It's pathetic," Other William said. "I'm talking to myself because there's nobody else around."

"There's nothing wrong with keeping myself company."

"Until it makes me desperate. I live alone. I'm miserable. I'm fawning over a ghost."

"You think you're fawning?"

"Don't you?"

"I think I'm helping her," I said. "And if it's really so pathetic talking to myself, focusing on June is good for me, too."

Other William frowned as if agreeing with my thought, as when a sharp, private insight cuts enough to sting. I wondered if he'd do the same, revealing me to me. I partly hoped he would but viscerally feared it.

"I assume our lives have been identical," I said. "The house is like a dream world full of possibility. The three-winged pigeon eats coffee beans. I think he's starting to like me. The couple in the kitchen seem to be in love. I tried to abort the camera trap I'd set for Mr. Gormly only to find he'd turned the tables. I felt I deserved it."

"Living here depresses me," Other William said. "The pigeon makes me anxious—I only feed it so it flies away—and every morning I watch a husband and wife mutilate each other over breakfast. As for Mr. Gormly, I've given serious thought to boarding up the door and trapping him in the basement. He's an intruder in my house and needs to learn his place."

Our vision had adapted to the room's nocturnal light and we watched each other closely, consoled by our familiar features but equally unsettled by a deep sense of foreignness.

"I've been wondering…"

"I know," he said. "But go ahead and ask."

"When June isn't here, is she over there with you?"

"If everything that happens here happens there, too," he said, "there must be two of her. June and Other June. When she vanishes from one side, she vanishes from both."

"If you and I are superficially identical but temperamentally different," I said, "are the Junes different, too?"

"Mine is elusive and depressed. She's also flirty and sweet."

"Mine is sweet and flirty. She's also depressed and elusive."

"So the question," Other William said, "is whether the two Junes' character traits are inverse reflections, or if *our* inversed perspectives are causing the apparent difference. We both agree she's selfish."

"I don't think that," I said.

I watched my own face repulse me with a sneer.

"She's bright, she's dark, she's here, she's gone. She leaves without considering the loneliness I'll suffer and, whether she's with me or not, she's constantly, obsessively the center of my attention."

"That's the whole point of being here."

"Is it?" Other William asked.

"What are you trying to say?"

"After all my care and effort, what have I learned? What has she shared?"

"She doesn't remember who she was."

"What about her coat-check story? She remembers all that but nothing else about her life? Look at how she slips around the most important questions. Even I have a pretty good guess at how she died and yet she claims she doesn't know."

"It's safer in the dark," I said, echoing her words.

"What if I needed her right now? Could I call her? Would she come?"

Rosemary-mint wafted from my shoes: a trace of the perfume I'd tracked around the house. I rubbed my neck where June had licked me—Other William did, too—and kept my hand against the pulse. I wanted to summon her and prove him wrong but didn't know how.

Other William looked at me with sad, jellied eyes.

"Remember the forest dream," he said.

On a night before my mother died, I'd dreamt that we were holding hands and walking in a pinewood. The light was grayish green, the needle bed was cushiony, and snow flurries gently fluttered up instead of falling. My mother pulled ahead of me without releasing my hand, as if the space between our bodies was distorting or distending. She was ten steps ahead, then a mile, then a lifetime. Our arms were like Silly Putty stretching to a thread until it snapped and my mother's half rippled out of sight.

"I came to find Mom," Other William said. "Instead I'm spending all my time focusing on June."

"You're wrong," I said, jarring his composure with my hardness. "I came to find closure and I found someone new."

"That's the heartache with June. She's someone new to lose."

I tried to forget the conversation by reading *The Spiral Grimoire*, the obscure old spellbook my mother had adored. I had studied it before, having acquired my own copy three years earlier, but I'd never succeeded in casting any of its spells. Maybe the book was full of nonsense, maybe I lacked the skill, or maybe my timidity had doomed every effort.

Whatever the reason for my failures, I hadn't yet tried in the brownstone's conducive atmosphere, and as I sat there missing June, sipping coffee touched with gin, I decided I would give the grimoire another go. I found a curious charm called the Viscera Perfuma, which was said to induce nostalgia for an unrequited love. The aim was not to injure but to conjure deep remembrance, beautified by time, of youthful brokenheartedness and bittersweet wisdom.

Mr. Gormly seemed an ideal target for the charm. I hoped if I could reignite a yearning from his past, he might be less icy and reclusive in the present.

The spell required concentration; an item from the subject (I used the crumpled note Mr. Gormly had left with his rent); and the petal of a rose, which I was required to chew throughout the incantation. In lieu of a fresh rose, I chewed a dried petal that had been pressed into one of my mother's photo albums. It tasted like tea made of funeral home flowers.

Only after finishing the spell did I realize I had no means of testing its success. Disheartened and vaguely ill, I rinsed my mouth, ate a tuna sandwich in the kitchen, and returned to my study to read. I napped and woke up bleary, having dreamt of falling light, and the room was sad and heavy with the onset of dusk. I drank a little less coffee and a little more gin. Night fell. The study's lamps emphasized the dark.

I played the radio to stop myself from listening to silence. A song I hadn't heard since high school reminded me of night drives around my hometown's starlit hills. I thought of pine-dark roads, meteors, and cornfields. I thought of swimming in a pond that was warmer than the air. I thought of a young woman's knee, nuzzled in my palm, and the ice-cream flavor at the corner of her mouth.

"Come back," I said. "Please. I need you here tonight."

Another hour passed and I was halfheartedly reading when an infestation of house centipedes scurried into the room, as quiet as a thousand-legged, undulating shadow.

The tension in my neck immediately eased. Years ago, I'd learned from an occult entomologist that house centipedes' antennae worked like lightning rods for negative psychic energy. A single centipede could neutralize the charge of a stressful thought, even one sizzling in the depths of the subconscious. Anecdotal evidence pointed to infestations reducing high blood pressure, suicidal tendencies, familial discord, and—in one obscure case—a malignant brain tumor in a seven-year-old girl.

I smiled as the influx spread around the study. The rug, walls, and ceiling quivered with delicate limbs. Such a prodigious brood made me suspect the presence of a queen, and I gingerly stepped out of the study, taking care not to crush my newfound companions, and crept around the house searching for their mother.

A surge of positive energy led me to the downstairs utility room. I opened the door and peaked inside, where two enormous antennae swayed in my direction from behind the ancient water tank. They were longer than my forearms and semi-translucent.

The queen rippled forward just enough to show her head. She was as tall as my knee and, judging by the tremor of her steps, somewhere in the realm of one hundred pounds. She remained uncannily still after her advance. If her tranquilizing presence hadn't put me so at ease, I would have been alarmed by her thick and venomous forcipules.

I slowly reached a finger out and touched her antenna.

"My house is your house," I said.

Her other antenna gently stroked my arm.

We regarded each other for five or ten minutes, peacefully together. Eventually I said good night, left her in the utility room, and returned to my study, where the hundreds of smaller centipedes cleared a path for me to walk.

It was the time of night when silence seems to fizz, as if the next day's flavor was beginning to ferment. Meeting the centipedes had given me a multi-limbed vivacity, and for the first time all night, my energy flowed out instead of flowing in.

I started tearing pages out of a book called *Splendorous Dark: Erotic Tales of Succubi and Witches through the Ages* and taping them onto the wall in sequential order. It was an offering to June, who couldn't flip through books but would able to read the taped-up pages if she reappeared in the study without me.

I had reservations about presenting that particular text for her enjoyment, but it was the only book, aside from *The Spiral Grimoire*, of which I possessed two copies. I needed a pair because the pages were double-sided; I used the first copy for even pages and the second for odd, so every sequential page was available to read.

Most of the centipedes had dispersed by the time I'd taped a hundred and ten pages to the wall. The expanse of white paper made the study brighter, and I went to my bedroom and quickly fell asleep, confident that June would be back the next day.

I woke in the dark, terrified and jarred.

My body and the brownstone trembled to their bones. There was something too unnatural in the rumbling for an earthquake. It was a sinister vibration that wasn't wholly physical but rather like a trembling of the spirit world around me.

The quakes began to soften—my sense of dread didn't—only to be replaced by hammering, clangs, and scrapes far below me. I heard a large metal object thudding onto its side. The sounds were dull but loud, like those of a demolition crew working in the basement, and I pictured Mr. Gormly as a vague, tiny shadow wielding oversized tools and undermining the house's foundation.

Adrenaline splashed my heart. I leapt out of bed in my boxers, grabbed my pocketlight, and donned a leather motorcycle helmet I'd salvaged from the oddments room for just such an emergency. I ran to the basement door and barreled downstairs, where I pulled the lightbulb cord, knowing the helmet would safeguard my hair from another round of Hungarian curlers. But no curlers fell, the bulb lit the basement around the bottom of the stairs, and I shined my pocketlight into the deeper, darker recesses, looking for Mr. Gormly.

The cacophony had stopped and I discovered no immediate wreckage, but the basement looked unusually bare, and it took me several seconds to realize that most of the old furniture and debris I'd seen earlier was gone. I proceeded slowly to Mr.

Gormly's corner, unnerved by the diminished but continuing tremors in the atmosphere, which had the premonitory feel of imminent explosion.

I stood amazed when my pocketlight revealed a manmade wall. Only "wall" was not the word. The structure was more of a rounded barricade rising from floor to ceiling and entirely surrounding Mr. Gormly's quarters. The basement's curious emptiness was instantly explained; the barricade had been constructed with tables and chairs, a ruined upright piano, cinder blocks, pipes, plaster board, rusted scrap metal, lamps, antique signage, and ancient boards that probably hadn't been used since the brownstone's construction in 1817. How he'd moved the larger items unassisted defied understanding, but I was far more concerned with knowing what he was up to.

"Gormly!" I said. "Come out here and face me!"

The house began to tremble again. My innards quaked. The air felt poisonous and thin, and either my pocketlight weakened or the dark turned darker.

An envelope shot through a fissure in the barricade, whisked past my face, and papercut my cheek. I tore it open and read the note.

Retreat.

Sincerely,
Mr. Gormly

Black smoke billowed from the barricade's base. I staggered back, stumbled on the uneven floor, and sat down roughly in a pothole of sludge. My heart felt saggy and my limbs went slack. The smoke expanded and surrounded me, blotting out of the basement, and its tendril-like wisps touched the edges of my brain. It seemed as if the smoke were pure emotion or a snuffing of my senses—a something, or a nothing, that my conscious mind retreated from.

"Gormly's killing me," I thought. "I'll be dead now, too."

My bedroom, my study with the taped-up pages, and the whole house above me felt hopelessly remote. And yet I didn't feel afraid. I simply didn't care. I drooped as if I'd always been depressed and always would be. Everything was dimming and my thoughts began to fade. Then I breathed a last sigh, emptying my lungs, and felt myself dissolve forever in the dark.

7. THE LIBRARY GARDEN

I came to my senses lying in the first-floor hallway. My leather helmet and pocketlight were next to me, the carpet runner was lichenous under my back, and a wall sconce glowed feebly overhead. I sat up abruptly and my brain seemed hesitant to rise, and when I looked to the end of the hall and saw the basement door was closed, my memory of the smoke almost made me sob.

June rubbed my arm.

"You're here," I said. "You're back."

Other William had been wrong—I'd needed her, she'd come—except I wasn't yet convinced that anything was real. My relief had the feeling of escaping from an evil dream, only to find that waking up had been another dream.

"YOU OK?" she asked. "WHAT HAPPENED? EVERYTHING SEEMED TO SHAKE."

"I don't know, I don't know. You felt the tremors, too?"

"I WAS IN THE STUDY, READING THE PAGES YOU PUT ON THE WALL. I SUDDENLY FELT THIS AWFUL KIND OF PANICKY VIBRATION. LIKE A NIGHTMARE SHUDDERING UP AND SWALLOWING THE HOUSE."

"How'd you get me out of the basement?"

"I FOUND YOU HERE ON THE FLOOR."

I palpated my body, especially the back of my head, but felt no lumps or soreness to indicate that Mr. Gormly had dragged me upstairs.

I knelt and faced in June's direction, drawing a breath that made my body feel tenuous and weightless, and braced against the wall to keep from slumping over.

"THERE'S SOMETHING ON YOUR SHIRT," she said.

A small, folded note was pinned above my heart. I opened it and read:

Do not enter the basement.

Sincerely,
Mr. Gormly

I was too drained to swear. I crumpled up the note and told June about the dreadful smoke from Mr. Gormly's barricade.

"It felt like death, or something worse, condensing all around me."

"WE NEED TO GO," June said. "I'M FEELING IT AGAIN."

She was right. Directly under the floorboards and joists, whatever it was intensified and pressed up toward us. I wobbled to my feet and walked toward the basement door, driven by a morbid curiosity to open it. I thought of Other William mirroring my movements as he made his way forward down his own dreary hall.

I reached the door and squeezed the oily brass knob. Oblivion, I thought, was one turn away: every question, every ache, every longing would be gone. If Other William opened his door, I would open mine, and we would disappear together like reflections lacking mirrors.

June swept her hands through the middle of my head, shuffling my thoughts like she was mussing my hair.

"STOP," she said. "WHATEVER YOU'RE THINKING ISN'T RIGHT."

Suddenly the basement felt deathly and abhorrent. I wiped my face hard as if to physically clear my thoughts.

"We can't leave Gormly alone down there. Even if he's responsible, the atmosphere could kill him."

"HE CARRIED YOU UP AND LEFT A NOTE. HE'S FINE."

"But what if he isn't?"

"LISTEN TO ME," she said. "THERE'S SOMEONE IN YOUR STUDY."

"What?"

"I'LL TELL YOU ONCE WE GO. IT'S BAD HERE FOR ME. I'M LEAVING WITH OR WITHOUT YOU."

I followed her up the hall and up the front staircase to the second-floor landing, where the basement's negative influence immediately lessened and the questions in my mind clarified and colorized. Before I could ask a thing, June was writing on my hand.

"THE QUAKES SCARED ME SO BAD, I'D HAVE PUKED IF I HAD GUTS. I LEFT THE STUDY AND DIDN'T SEE ANYTHING WEIRD IN THE HALL, BUT WHEN I LOOKED BACK AT THE ROOM, THERE WAS A DOORWAY IN THE DOORWAY. LIKE A HALF OPEN DOOR MADE OF NOTHING. MADE OF AIR. IT LED SOMEWHERE ELSE, OTHER THAN THE STUDY. THERE WAS A GARDEN FULL OF FERNS AND SKYLIGHT AND BOOKS. A LITTLE OLD MAN WAS STANDING IN THE GARDEN. HE TOLD ME THE HOUSE WASN'T SAFE AND I SHOULD COME INSIDE AND WAIT UNTIL THE DANGER WENT

AWAY. EXCEPT HE DIDN'T REALLY TALK."

"What do you mean?"

"I CAN'T EXPLAIN IT. I SAID I COULDN'T STAY, I HAD TO FIND YOU. HE SAID IF WE SURVIVED, THE TWO OF US SHOULD VISIT HIM. HE SAID HE'D LEAVE THE DOOR OPEN TILL WE CAME."

Predawn light from the window near the staircase made me realize just how much I'd experienced since dusk the previous day: the Viscera Perfuma spell, the centipedes, the smoke, and now a stranger in a garden where a garden couldn't be. I'd been unconscious and was only mostly certain I'd awakened.

"Show me," I said, starting down the hall toward my study.

"WAIT," June said. "I NEED TO TELL YOU SOMETHING AWFUL."

She paused and rubbed my hand until I felt a phantom warmth.

"WHEN I SAW YOU ON THE FLOOR, I ALMOST HOPED YOU'D DIED. I THOUGHT IF YOU WERE A GHOST, IT'D BE EASIER FOR ME."

The dawn light was pale with blurry hints of pink, as if the day itself were bloodshot and falling back asleep. I was nearly too saddened and exhausted to reply.

"That's understandable," I said. "I wish you had a body and you wish I was a ghost. We want to share space like everybody else."

"I'M SORRY ANYWAY. I'M GLAD YOU'RE NOT DEAD."

"So am I. But we're together now."

"PLUS THERE'S SOMEONE NEW," June said.

We stood in the hall outside my study, where the open

doorway showed the familiar room with its dawn-lit bookcases, a smattering of centipedes enlivening the floor, and the torn pages I had crookedly taped across the wall.

"There's nothing here," I said.

"LOOK CLOSER AT THE DOORWAY."

In the left half of the open space, there was a thin, vertical line I'd noticed but dismissed as a trick of early sunlight. At the top and bottom, the line extended horizontally at right angles and formed what appeared to be the gap around an invisible, slightly ajar door. I slipped my fingers into the gap and pulled the door open.

In place of the ordinary room, I saw a dense, peculiar garden. Stepping in was like stepping into someone else's dream.

The garden's square-footage was identical to that of my study, but there were tightly packed trees and ferns instead of walls, and a sense of infinite space sprawling out beyond them. The floor consisted of moss and rich, chocolatey soil. A cobbled path led across the clearing to the farthest vegetation. Instead of a plastered ceiling, a cobalt sky glimmered with the evening's first bright stars, and the atmosphere was soft with luscious greens and violets. Winter had turned to summer and dawn had changed to dusk.

A table stood in the middle of the garden. So many books were heaped on top and underneath it, I knew it was a table only from the shape. A version of my reading chair—green instead of red—was stationed to the left and hemmed by stacks of earth-toned volumes. I began to notice books everywhere. They were tucked into shelves hidden in the flora, mounded into stratified rock formations, and even underfoot where the covers, spines, and pages were partially revealed beneath the moss and dirt.

June touched my hand and I instinctively knew where she

wanted me to look. In the back right corner of the garden, plainly visible, was a man I had somehow overlooked until that moment.

He seemed to walk toward us, placing one foot in front of the other and drawing steadily closer, but when he finally stood before us, I discovered he hadn't approached us. Somehow the two of us had moved toward him.

He was short, rising only to the level of my chin, with narrow shoulders and delicate limbs. He looked ancient, as if he'd lived a long time and kept aging after death. He had thick, silver hair and a sharp spade beard, and his clear round eyes were childlike and kind. His lunar skin, wrinkles, and arthritically twisted joints were curiously fluid, and his body—though apparently that of a withered old man—was as changeable and graceful as a watery reflection.

He was unabashedly naked, not like someone who'd forgotten he wasn't dressed, but like someone who'd forgotten all the shame about his body. I was nevertheless distracted by the man's full exposure. I also started wondering if June was naked, too.

She herself remained invisible to me, but apparently the old man could see her, because he smiled at where she stood and said:

Peachy, quick and here again. Welcome, dears, welcome. I've been reading since the beaver moon. It's good to rest my brain, figuratively speaking, and meet someone living outside a book.

Only he didn't make a sound. He expressed himself silently, with what I would inadequately describe as a form of charades. His body remained like that of an old man even as it morphed into contortionist shapes that defied logic: a two-legged figure with seven legs, a face made of hands, a skeleton I couldn't see but knew was forming symbols. He floated and coiled without actually moving. He was animated hieroglyphs, cuneiform, or runes—an alphabet of nuance and quality and tone—and just as he had seemed to approach us when we'd moved toward him, his meaning was conveyed by shaping our perspectives.

Even a word such as "peachy" was immediately clear. I understood him perfectly. June did, too.

Several seconds passed before he spoke again to June.

You're welcome, he said. *I'm tickled you enjoy it. I've been dreaming it for years. You should see it in the winter with the caroling snow and glowbirds.*

"He can hear you when you talk?" I asked June.

"I SORT OF THINK AT HIM," she said.

"What did you think?"

"I THANKED HIM FOR LEAVING THE DOOR AJAR AND SAID I LIKE HIS GARDEN."

We quickly agreed that she would write her words to me in my palm, and her words to the old man on the back of my hand, allowing me to understand the three-way conversation.

"I'M JUNE," she told the man. "THIS IS MY FRIEND WILLIAM. HE OWNS THE HOUSE."

Warmed to meet you both, he said. *My name is Leonard Stick.*

"Mr. Stick!" I said, so forcefully his whole figure rippled. "My last name is Rook. You knew my mother Charlotte."

Mr. Stick expressed a wordless geyser of delight, intermingled with compassion and a deep, nostalgic sadness. My inner self shifted, mirroring the shapes he outwardly embodied. June sidled up close and braced me with her arm. It felt as if she truly would have caught me if I fell.

"You know what happened to her," I said.

In part, and partly not, he said. *I'm infinitely sorry. She was a friend—a kindred light—and I was heartsick to lose her.*

Memories enshrouded me, unique but intersewn. Walking to school with my mother over ice-crisped leaves. The softness of her shea-buttered hands. Night TV. Chewing marshmallows, dry and stiff, from powdered hot cocoa. All the warmth, all the nourishment of kissing her goodnight.

I was straw and brittle leaves by the time I met your mother, Mr. Stick said. *She helped me find many lost books, rare and strange. When my seams began to rupture and I couldn't leave the house, she visited and helped me find one last book—the rarest and the strangest. One I desperately required.*

"*The Book of Elements,*" I said. "My mother talked about that."

Yes! It comes as water, earth, flame, or air depending on the reader. The text is comprehensible to anyone who summons it, but after one use, it vanishes again and nobody who reads it can remember what it said.

"IF EVERYONE FORGETS," June said, "HOW DO YOU KNOW IT EXISTS?"

The effects of its use are easily remembered. Scads of stories appear in occult literature. A father in medieval France appeared as rain to his three daughters, simultaneously in different locations, to impart a special warning that apparently saved their lives. A Russian child, lost in the boreal forest, survived by summoning the book and transforming himself into a wolf. In Vermont, a woman impregnated herself with herself, died giving birth to herself, and lived a second life as her own infant daughter. Other uses have been grimmer. Suicide, insanity, torture—sometimes afflicting enemies, other times rebounding on the user. Like any book, he said, *it's a heart made to pump whatever blood the reader fills it with.*

"What did you do with it?" I asked.

I was a lifelong occultist devoted to the otherworld. The

borderlines enthralled me, not the absolute beyond. When I learned I was dying, I was hesitant to go, and so I used the book to stay in the house instead of moving onward. My place is at the threshold. I haunt it voluntarily. As both of you can see, I communicate easily with those on either side—those with bodies, those without. I had hoped to talk longer, much longer, with your mother.

The garden's light had fallen to a late-dusk blandness, neither as colorful as evening nor as velvety as night. Mr. Stick's indescribable contortions, already as natural to me as regular speech, became more difficult to follow without intense concentration, like the gray-on-gray words of cheaply printed paperbacks. I stayed close to June, wishing I could clutch her arm and worried she would fade along with everything else around me.

"What happened to my mother?"

Please believe me, Mr. Stick said. *I never wished her harm. She helped me summon the book. It came to me as air: a volume made of breezes, balmy and refreshing. We were together when I used it. She was with me when I died.*

I had prearranged my cremation and the execution of my estate, and I had begged your mother to visit the house after I was dead, assuring her I'd find a way to talk with her again. She came and sat alone, faithful in the quiet, when I hadn't yet discovered how to make myself known. There's a learning curve in death, however one has died, that's almost as dramatic as the curve when we're born. I found a way to speak before she lost hope, although I have to say, your mother was a marvelous believer.

Once we finally reconnected, she listened to me for hours and days, thrilling me with questions I had scarcely thought to ask. I told her what I felt and learned. When I began to dream my library garden, one page and seed at a time, I grew so preoccupied I sometimes ignored her. Never purposely, but nonetheless. My ego had survived, with all its sucking mouths, and I didn't notice your mother had started to summon The Book of Elements herself.

It came to her as water, as a book made of snow. I saw it scatter into flurries after she had used it. Only after, though—past the point of warning or advising her. She wanted to see what I was seeing, to share in my experience. She didn't try to die. She merely cleared a view, squeegeeing the muck off the glass, so to speak. You need to understand, she didn't know what she was doing. She suddenly saw the world and the otherworld together. The visions overwhelmed her and she wandered from the house, boggled and amazed and lost inside herself.

The trees sagged toward me like the ceiling of a blanket fort. I used to sit for hours with a flashlight and books, with a fabric-softened canopy and pillows on the floor, knowing I could daydream and always come back. All I had to do was peek to see my room again. My mother had done the opposite. She'd peeked through a gap and lost sight of what was solid, comprehensible, and clear.

"Why did she need the book if she was already in the house?" I asked. "Something otherworldly happens every day here."

Those are peepholes and flickerlights. Your mother wanted more.

"You've seen more and haven't lost your mind."

I was dead. Your mother wasn't. Heavy gray brains are for heavy gray things, and when she saw beyond the physical world, her physical mind revolted. Your mother's double vision was a chaos of color. I don't believe she suffered, though. Not as you imagine. She may have been confused, but there are pleasures in confusion.

He smiled and the ferns, and even the air, smiled with him. Everything around us seemed to hint at secret meanings. Insects sang in throaty, blended chords. The garden's leaves were hands and books, opening and closing, and the stars' clear twinkles had telegraphic rhythms.

"Is she here?" I asked.

No.

"Is there any way to find her?"

Mr. Stick twisted like an alphabet of riddles, as elegant and baffling as a knot made of knots.

Meeting you is the closest I've ever come to finding your mother, he said. *Everybody dies as uniquely as they live. Some are easy to discover. Others stay hidden. There's no way to reach her if she doesn't reach back.*

So much of what I'd clung to was spiderwebs and fog. It was as if my mother's ghost had been with me for years, sustaining me without my ever knowing she was there, and in the instant I'd discovered her again, she'd disappeared. My bones turned soft, my blood felt tired, and my body seemed leached of nutrients and light. The garden's trees and stars were gray and indistinct, like any plain trees and any old stars. I smelled the basement's smoke again—a residue, I thought, in my nostrils or my brain— and wanted it to blot everything away.

June surprised me when she asked Mr. Stick a question, writing on my hand so I knew what she was saying. For minutes, I'd essentially forgotten she was with me.

"HOW ARE YOU A GHOST?" she asked.

I thought you understood. I used The Book of Elements.

"YEAH, BUT HOW EXACTLY?"

Given the nature of the book, I don't quite remember.

"GUESS," June said.

Mr. Stick softly fluttered.

There's a natural way of death, he said. *It comes to you, you face a choice, you move to what you choose. The book contained words that let me pick my afterlife. My choice to haunt the house would be terrible to most—a phantom life of solitude. It's paradise to me.*

"IT'S HELL TO ME," she said. "WHY AM I HERE? WHY AM I TRAPPED? I DIDN'T USE THE BOOK BUT NOW I'M STUCK THIS WAY, TOO."

You must have chosen it, my dear. Part of you wanted to remain.

The ferns hunched forward with carnivorous attention, and the stars sparked and sputtered like bulbs with faulty wires. Mr. Stick and I shivered from a vibratory chill. Was it possible that June was altering the garden? She was more than just invisible; she radiated dark.

"I DIDN'T WANT TO BE A GHOST."

May I ask how you died?

"I DON'T REMEMBER."

That's unusual, Mr. Stick said. I*nessential memories often disappear, but strong experiences—works, pains, loves, birth and death—are quintessential to your self. Do you ever slip briefly into dimness or unconsciousness?*

Her radiating darkness seemed to draw itself inward, and the garden warmed and swayed as if forgetting its distemper.

"She vanishes a lot," I said. "For hours. Sometimes days."

Mr. Stick's shape became a dreadful, wordless question that was something like a vortex, deep and self-devouring. June gripped my hand repeatedly and futilely.

However you came to this, he said, *however fiercely you resent it, you have to find ways to move in your existence. Was your ordinary life really any different with its fears, limitations, and mysterious design? Even limbo has options. With or without a body, you can actively imagine how to be here now.*

"I NEED THE BOOK OF ELEMENTS TO CHOOSE A WAY FORWARD."

The book is physical, he said. *You're a ghost. You couldn't summon it.*

"WILLIAM COULD," she said.

Mr. Stick warmed like a sun-struck cloud.

He looked at me and said, *She's right. You could do it. I trust you own a copy of The Spiral Grimoire? Like the Bible, it's a common text of uncommon depth, as endless as a fathomer's ability to fathom.*

June's energy ignited, same as Mr. Stick's. Together they produced an iridescent charge that made me feel as solid as a damp lump of clay.

"I'm an amateur with spells," I said.

Your mother was, too, but spells are simpler to accomplish inside the house. And expertise is less important than the underlying force— the will, or rather the Williamness, that you alone possess. Call the elements in turn, to or from yourself. Just remember when you summon the book, it does whatever you choose. Be careful which half of you decides how to use it.

"IT CAN REALLY DO ANYTHING?" June asked.

Anything that's possible. That's not to say everything is possible, he said, *but who am I to say what's impossible or not?*

"IF IT GETS ME OUT OF LIMBO, WHAT'S BEYOND ALL THIS?"

If we knew, we'd only wonder what's beyond all that. Mysteries are houses made of deeper, weirder houses. I'm satisfied exploring. Don't you love a good question? Ah! he said, pointing at the sky behind my head, as if a meteor were hurtling toward me with an answer.

I looked where he pointed but the stars looked secure. When I turned back to face him, he was suddenly at his table and the night draped around him as he hunched toward his books.

Something's dawning on me now, he said. *I need to read and think.*

"THANK YOU," June said. "I'M SORRY I WAS PUSHY."

You're welcome, and you weren't. You're a strawberry, dear.

"How do we talk to you again?" I asked.

You can't until I dream another door. Goodbye! Be good!

He opened a book and concentrated, huddled like an ordinary naked old man with his question-mark spine and frizzled silver hair. As his focus turned away from us, the garden dimmed and thinned and I began to see traces of my study in the corners.

June touched my hand and said, "THE TREES ARE FULL OF POLAROIDS."

Every leaf was black and thick, swaying in a breeze I believed but couldn't feel, and when I stared at one of the leaves I saw a picture blush through. I focused on the skin tone and thought I saw my mother. Whatever leaf I looked at steadily developed into a photograph I recognized from memorized exposures. June did the same and soon the trees were full of pictures, all of them evocative and blurry and elusive. The photographs of June—her features and her life—distracted me from clarifying any of my own until my mind was overwhelmed by countless fluttering images.

I felt as if the trees were made of soft, shifting pixels that would suddenly resolve into one perfect vision. But the photos wouldn't sharpen, either singly or together, and eventually a glow behind the trees pressed through. Colors paled. The leaves thinned and everything dissolved. Mr. Stick was gone. The garden had reverted to my study with its ordinary light and heavy brick walls.

"WOW," June said.

She weaved her fingers through my fingers. I squinted at the air and tried to see the photographs, exactly as I used to look for ghosts when I was young, but the plainness of the study dampened my amazement, and I closed my eyes and tried squinting inward for a while.

"I'M SORRY ABOUT YOUR MOM."

She was vital and electric, so solidly beside me that I looked in her direction, half-expecting I would see her. For much of the conversation we had shared with Mr. Stick, I'd all but let her vanish with my own preoccupations. I focused on her now, the way I'd focused on the Polaroids, trying to discover some better resolution.

"HEY. ARE YOU OK?"

"We need to summon the book," I said.

8. SUMMONING AIR AND FIRE

We sat in my study with *The Spiral Grimoire* open in my lap. I felt June's hair near the stubble on my cheek while I paged through, looking for a spell to summon air.

"YOU CAN READ THIS?" she asked, referring to the book's cryptic hodgepodge of symbols, illustrations, and languages ranging from Arabic to Uzbek and, here and there, ones that scholars had yet to identify. Much of the text was English, but even those pages were often abstruse or presented in a kind of esoteric shorthand.

"You can usually figure it out or fudge an understanding," I said, though honestly my thoughts were so disarrayed, all I wanted was to doze, undreaming, next to June.

I found what I believed to be an air-summoning spell. It was unnamed, or rather named with only a symbol: seven concentric circles of diminishing thickness, the innermost of which was virtually a dot. The spell itself was a single unintelligible word that ran for seven pages and was meant to be spoken loudly at a specific open space. Any space would do, as far as I could tell, but the word's exact pronunciation was unknowable and I was daunted by the breadth of unbroken letters.

"I'm supposed to say the word without pausing. I don't see how that's possible."

"MAYBE THE AIR FILLS YOUR LUNGS AND HELPS YOU FINISH," June said.

My stomach churned. I hadn't eaten since the previous day, and I was so beyond hunger, the thought of food revolted me. It left me feeling stupidly divided from myself, as if my mind was denying things my body needed.

"I've only tried few of these spells. I don't know what I'm doing."

"ONE WAY TO LEARN."

"I really need to force myself to eat and get some sleep. Plus I think I ought to do some research first. I have at least a dozen books that cover the fundamentals—basic techniques, warnings, transmundane safety measures."

"PLEASE," June said. "LET'S TRY IT ONCE NOW."

"What if I do it wrong?"

"YOU'LL SUMMON APOCALYPIC FORCES AND CHANGE REALITY FOREVER BECAUSE YOU'RE SUCH A POWERFUL SPELLCASTER. COME ON, IT'LL BE FUN. YOU'RE DOING MAGIC. THAT'S INSANE."

"OK. I'll give it a try."

"BE CONFIDENT AND BOLD AND PSYCH YOURSELF UP."

I closed my eyes and tried to feel the necessary verve, and then I gulped the last of my coffee, clanked down the mug, and left *The Spiral Grimoire* open on the floor. I stood and stretched my arms, dizzy from the sudden rise, and did a dozen jumping jacks to energize myself.

"Summon air. Summon air," I thought, picturing myself amid a swirl of rushing wind. I picked up the book and focused on my breathing.

"YOU CAN DO THIS," she said. "MAKE YOUR MOM PROUD."

Despite her good intention, I resented her for saying it and drew a vast breath as if to shout instead of talk. My lungs were so full, my shirt buttons strained. I stared at the book and started to read the seven-page word, aiming my voice, if not my eyes, toward the middle of the study.

"CLEARER," June said.

She wrote it on the back of my hand—the one I was using as a pointer, with my index finger following the word—and in the moment of distraction, I may have skipped a syllable or two. I carried on, losing breath but trying to recover.

"RELAX," June said.

I skipped a whole line because of her second interruption, but I couldn't go back without starting over and I couldn't tell June her advice wasn't helping. I zeroed into the spell, into the sound, into myself.

Half-a-page done, six-and-a-half to go.

I thought of breath control in singing—something about opening a space below my voice—and when my breath ran out, I gasped and tried to fill the space and kept speaking the word with scarcely any pause.

My heartrate slowed. A balmy peacefulness infused me and I needed less oxygen and effort to continue. The spell was meditation, I began to understand: a longwinded sound that was almost like silence as it quieted my thoughts and seemed to go forever.

Had I turned the page once, or was it twice? It didn't matter. I felt like Mr. Stick contorting into language. The word was in my body, and my body became the word, and I partly understood with mesmerized awareness that my eyes had left the book and yet I hadn't stopped reading. The word I spoke was obvious and effortless and strong, flowing like a long, bold note from a horn.

When I tried another gasp, the word wouldn't let me. My eyesight narrowed, my skin prickled coldly, and my lungs sagged and shriveled like old, dead balloons. I pounded on my chest, breathing out and out, steadily exhaling and expending and deflating.

Then the word stopped flowing and the sound disappeared. There was vacancy and quiet like the silence after music, and memories that didn't talk, and ghosts that couldn't listen.

"BREATHE," June said.

I swore I heard her voice.

I inhaled without thinking, easily and cleanly, and a whirlwind of oxygen and noise flooded into me. Colors flared. I felt my blood surging through my core with warmth and vigor and I opened up my mouth to breathe more richly. The air produced a vibratory humming in my throat, like the very lowest tones of a deeply drawn harmonica.

Wind swept the room, rushing in toward my lungs. It fluttered the pages I'd taped to the wall, and many of the pages snapped free and flew toward me. I swatted them away but the wind kept building, moving papers, notes, and burnt wooden matches off my desk. Lighter items soared directly at my mouth, including cobwebs and dust bunnies, some of which I fended off, some of which I swallowed. The massive inhalation felt natural and grand, as if the air itself adored me and was desperate to inflate me.

I turned away from June and kept my face toward the window.

I was afraid I'd breathe her in. I longed to breathe her in.

My curtains floated sideways, tethered to their rods like heavy green flags. Suction broke the windows, glass exploded everywhere, and powdery bursts of snow sparkled off the windowsill. Shocking cold air billowed into the study and equalized the pressure.

My lungs were finally full. I coughed a little cough and everything was still. The room was a catastrophe of papers and debris, much of which had gathered in a ring around my shoes.

"WILLIAM?" June said.

"I summoned air."

"YOU SUMMONED AIR! THAT WAS INCREDIBLE. AMAZING! YOU LOOKED LIKE MUNCH'S SCREAM BREATHING IN INSTEAD OF OUT."

"I summoned air," I said again, marveling at the normalcy of ordinary speech.

"HOW DO YOU FEEL?" she asked.

"Full. Like I'm bigger inside. Except it's almost like…"

"WHAT?"

"Like I swallowed something bad."

I rubbed my gut and felt a minor stab behind my navel. I hoped it wasn't glass. The pain subsided under the pressure of my fingers. Only gas, I thought.

"I can't believe I did it first try."

"MR. STICK SAID YOUR MOTHER HAD A KNACK," June said. "MAYBE YOU DO, TOO."

"*The Book of Elements* didn't appear." I toed through the heaps of blown papers at my feet. "I guess I didn't really think a single spell would do it."

"WE'LL NEED THE OTHER ELEMENTS. MAYBE TWO AT ONCE, IF WE CAN FIGURE OUT… LOOK!"

"What?" I said. "Where?"

"THE PIGEON'S UNDER YOUR DESK."

He must have gotten sucked into the study when the window broke. I knelt amid the debris to get a better view. He bobbled out from under my desk chair, fixed me with a beady eye, and raised his extra wing.

"IS HE HURT?" June asked.

"I don't think so," I said. "But there's something in his beak."

I started crawling closer but immediately stopped when he puffed himself up with predatory bluster.

"Maybe you can get closer."

The pigeon didn't notice June's invisible approach, and I remained uncomfortably still on all fours until she returned to my side and said, "IT'S A KEY. MADE OF BONE."

The pigeon bobbled farther into the center of the room and I could see the little key clamped in his beak. The key's stem was like a fish rib. Its teeth were like teeth.

I made a move toward him and he flapped into flight, taking the key and leaving downy gray feathers on the floor. We watched him fly away, out the window, out of sight.

"HUH," June said.

My stomach pain returned.

I forced myself to eat toast, drank a pint of cold water, and slept until the afternoon. June stayed with me. I woke up physically refreshed but otherwise stunned, as if my subconscious mind had also been asleep and all of my awareness had the same stupefaction. I didn't remember coming to the room and going to bed. It took me several minutes, staring at the ceiling, not only to recall what Mr. Stick had said but also to believe we'd met the man at all. The house, and June beside me, felt both familiar and mysteriously changed.

"I HAD A DREAM," June said.

I rolled to face her just as naturally as if she had a face.

"I THINK IT'S A MEMORY OF MY LIFE, BUT I

CAN'T TELL WHAT PARTS OF IT ARE REAL. IT ALL FELT TRUE BUT IT ALL FELT DREAMED."

"What was it about?"

"I'M TRYING TO THINK HOW IT STARTED. YOU KNOW THE WAY DREAMS HAPPEN OUT OF ORDER BUT IT STILL MAKES SENSE? THERE'S ALL THE CONTEXT NO ONE BUT THE DREAMER UNDERSTANDS."

"Just tell me what you remember."

"I WAS A SENIOR IN HIGH SCHOOL AND HAD A GIRLFRIEND."

"Is that part true?"

"NO, I'M STRAIGHT," June said. "MY DREAM GIRLFRIEND MUST HAVE BEEN A STAND-IN FOR AN ACTUAL BOYFRIEND. OR NONE OF IT HAPPENED, I DON'T KNOW. HER NAME WAS ISOBEL BUT EVERYONE CALLED HER IZZY. WE FELL IN LOVE IN OCTOBER AND DATED SENIOR YEAR. WE LIVED CLOSE ENOUGH TO WALK TO EACH OTHER'S HOUSES MOST NIGHTS. MY PARENTS LOVED HER AND HERS LOVED ME. WE WENT TO PROM. WE SURVIVED HIGH SCHOOL AND GRADUATED TOGETHER. AND THEN WE PICKED DIFFERENT COLLEGES EIGHT-HUNDRED-AND-NINETY-TWO MILES APART BUT DIDN'T SEE THE DISTANCE AS A THREAT.

"WE JOKED ABOUT GETTING MARRIED SOMEDAY. WHEN THE JOKES BECAME TALKS, THEY WERE SHORT BUT REALLY EXCITING, LIKE TEASERS FOR A MOVIE BOTH OF US IMAGINED.

"IZZY HAD A TWIN BROTHER NAMED RYAN OR

BRIAN. I'LL CALL HIM BRIAN. THEY RESEMBLED EACH OTHER A TON. THEY HAD THE SAME CHARM AND OPTIMISM. SAME SENSE OF HUMOR. THEIR CLOSENESS WAS THE ONLY THING THAT EVER MADE ME FEEL LIKE AN OUTSIDER IN IZZY'S LIFE. BUT BRIAN AND I GOT ALONG AWESOME. HE TEASED ME LIKE A BROTHER AND I MADE FUN OF HIS CLOTHES. HE WAS ALWAYS GIVING ME PIECES OF GLOW-IN-THE-DARK GUM HE KEPT IN HIS POCKET. ONE TIME IZZY SAID BRIAN WOULD HAVE BEEN MY IDEAL BOYFRIEND IF I'D BEEN BORN STRAIGHT IN SOME ALTERNATE DIMENSION. I LOVED THINKING HE'D BE MY BROTHER-IN-LAW SOMEDAY."

"Maybe *he* was your real boyfriend and the dream switched things around," I said.

"MAYBE. DOESN'T MATTER. IN MY DREAM, I LOVED IZZY AND THAT'S WHERE THE EMOTION WAS. SO ALL OF THAT WAS BACKGROUND TO THE DREAM, JUST STUFF I KNEW WHEN THE DREAM REALLY STARTED. I WAS HAPPY LOVING IZZY. DEEPLY, SAFELY HAPPY, CHEWING GLOW-IN-THE-DARK GUM.

"THEN THE GUM TURNED WEIRD AND IT WAS A WEDNESDAY NIGHT, AT 11:31 P.M., IN THE MIDDLE OF JULY. BRIAN WAS DRIVING HOME FROM HIS JOB AT THE MALL. HE WASN'T DRUNK. HE WASN'T SPEEDING OR USING HIS PHONE. BUT AT THIS WELL-KNOWN BEND A QUARTER-MILE FROM HIS HOUSE, HE LOST CONTROL OF HIS CAR, HIT AN ELM TREE, AND DIED.

"I WAS HOME IN THE BATHTUB AND WONDERED ABOUT THE SIRENS. IZZY WAS HOME IN HER ROOM, CLOSE ENOUGH TO HEAR THE CRASH. SHE CALLED ME AFTER MIDNIGHT. I'D BEEN WEARING PAJAMAS IN THE TUB AND THEY WERE SO HEAVY. IT TOOK ME FOREVER TO GET TO MY PHONE, AND BY THE TIME I ANSWERED I REALIZED WE'D ALREADY HAD THE CONVERSATION AND IZZY HAD BEEN CRYING.

"THE REST OF THE NIGHT AND THE NEXT DAY SMEARED TOGETHER. I KEPT TRYING TO GET A HOLD OF IZZY BUT SHE WOULDN'T ANSWER TEXTS OR CALLS, AND IT DROVE ME CRAZY KNOWING HER FAMILY WAS TOGETHER AND I FELT LIKE I BELONGED THERE, TOO. EVENTUALLY I WALKED TO HER HOUSE AND THERE WERE THESE UNFAMILIAR RELATIVES STANDING ON HER PORCH. THEY ALL HAD THE SAME FACE AND NONE OF THEM LOOKED AT ME. I FELT LIKE I WAS AT A STRANGER'S HOUSE, AND THE SUNLIGHT WAS BAD AND MADE THE TREES AND GRASS A COLOR I WASN'T USED TO.

"IZZY'S DAD CAME OUT AND MET ME ON THE LAWN. HE SEEMED LIKE A COPY OF THE MAN I REALLY KNEW. LIKE AN UNREHEARSED ACTOR HAD BEEN HIRED FOR THE PART OF A GRIEVING DAD. I STARTED CRYING WHEN I SAW HIM. I WANTED TO HUG HIM, AND I WANTED THE PEOPLE ON THE PORCH TO SEE ME AS IMPORTANT.

"HE KNEW I WAS THERE FOR IZZY AND SAID,

'SHE'S SLEEPING NOW.' HE MADE IT SOUND LIKE IZZY WAS THE ONE WHO'D REALLY DIED. I DIDN'T KNOW WHAT TO SAY. I WANTED IN, I NEEDED IZZY, AND I HUGGED HIM HARD AND SOBBED ON HIS CHEST. WHEN HE DIDN'T CRY BACK, I PULLED AWAY AND FELT EMBARRASSED. THE RELATIVES ON THE PORCH WERE WATCHING US BUT NOBODY WAS TALKING. I ASKED IF I COULD COME INSIDE AND WAIT UNTIL IZZY WOKE UP.

"'IT'S FAMILY NOW,' HE SAID. MEANING NO, BECAUSE I WASN'T.

"HE PROMISED IZZY WOULD CALL ME LATER. I DON'T REMEMBER WALKING HOME, OR TALKING TO MY PARENTS, OR ANYTHING ELSE ABOUT THE DAY EXCEPT FOR HATING IZZY'S FATHER AND HATING MYSELF FOR FEELING THAT WAY.

"BUT IZZY CALLED ME THAT NIGHT AND WE TALKED AND CRIED TOGETHER FOR HOURS, AND I WENT TO HER HOUSE THE NEXT DAY AND CRIED WITH HER PARENTS, TOO, AND EVERYTHING FELT RIGHT ABOUT MY PLACE IN IZZY'S LIFE. SHE CLUNG TO ME DURING THE FUNERAL.

"I HAD THIS SELFISH FEELING THROUGH IT ALL. I WOULDN'T CALL IT ENJOYMENT. I WAS CRUSHED THAT BRIAN WAS DEAD. BUT I FELT LIKE HIS DEATH HAD BROUGHT ME AND IZZY PERMANENTLY TOGETHER. WE SHARED A TRAGEDY, YOU KNOW? NO MATTER WHAT HAPPENED FOR THE REST OF OUR LIVES, I'D ALWAYS BE THE ONE WHO SHARED HER BROTHER'S DEATH.

"BUT THAT'S EXACTLY WHAT WRECKED US. AFTER THE FUNERAL, IZZY WAS MANIC. LIKE CONSTANTLY BUSY AND THROWING HERSELF INTO LIFE TO HONOR BRIAN'S MEMORY OR WHATEVER. SHE TOOK DANCING LESSONS, COOKED THESE HUGE COLORFUL DINNERS FOR HER PARENTS, STARTED HANGING WITH COUSINS SHE HADN'T TALKED TO IN YEARS. SHE WENT ON DAY TRIPS, WENT TO FESTIVALS, VISITED MUSEUMS. SOMETIMES WITH ME BUT MORE AND MORE WITHOUT ME. I HAD THIS FEELING SHE ASSOCIATED ME WITH BRAIN'S DEATH. LIKE SHE WOULD LOOK AT ME AND SEE HERSELF GRIEVING. I HAD THIS FEELING THAT I LITERALLY SMELLED LIKE A FUNERAL.

"IT HURT LIKE HELL BUT I GAVE HER SPACE. I WOULDN'T TELL HER WHAT SHE COULD OR COULDN'T DO, HOW TO CHANGE, OR HOW TO BE, BUT WHENEVER WE WERE TOGETHER, WE ONLY REALLY TALKED ABOUT TWO THINGS: BRIAN'S DEATH AND LIFE IN COLLEGE. WHAT HAD HAPPENED, WHAT WAS COMING. WE DIDN'T HAVE ANYTHING TOGETHER RIGHT NOW.

"THIS ONE PART OF THE DREAM... I THINK IT ACTUALLY CAME FIRST WHEN I WAS DREAMING, OUT OF ORDER. LIKE I ALREADY KNEW THE END AS SOON AS IT BEGAN. IZZY AND I WERE TOGETHER AND I TOLD HER EVERYTHING THAT HURT. HOW WE ALMOST NEVER KISSED ANYMORE. HOW I COULDN'T PLAY A BAND WE BOTH LIKED BECAUSE SHE'D GONE TO THE CONCERT WITH

HER COUSINS AND DIDN'T TAKE ME. HOW I
STARTED EVERY TEXT EXCHANGE. HOW SHE
DIDN'T EVEN CRY ABOUT BRIAN IN FRONT OF ME
ANYMORE. SHE EITHER CRIED ALONE OR CRIED
WITH OTHER PEOPLE.

"AND THEN SHE WAS OFF TO COLLEGE AND
THE TWO OF US WERE DONE.

"I WENT TO THE TREE WHERE BRIAN CRASHED.
PEOPLE HAD MADE A SHRINE WITH FLOWERS
AND CARDS AND CANDLES AROUND THE TRUNK.
I'D LEFT SOMETHING, TOO. IT WAS A PICTURE
OF ME, BRIAN, AND IZZY. HE WAS HEADLOCKING
BOTH OF US AND ALL OF US WERE LAUGHING.
THE FLOWERS HAD WILTED AND THE CARDS
HAD FALLEN APART IN THE RAIN, BUT I'D LEFT MY
PICTURE IN A PLASTIC SHEET TO KEEP IT SAFE.
THE WHOLE MEMORIAL WAS A MESS EXCEPT
FOR THAT PICTURE, AND SEEING US PRESERVED
SO PERFECTLY WAS AWFUL.

"I TOOK THE PICTURE OUT OF THE PLASTIC,
CHEWED A PIECE OF THE GLOW-IN-THE-DARK
GUM, AND SPAT IT AT THE PICTURE. IT BOUNCED
OFF AND DIMMED. AND THEN I KEPT CHEWING
NEW PIECES OF GUM AND SPITTING THEM OUT,
OVER AND OVER, AND I STOPPED BEING ANGRY
AND JUST WANTED ONE OF THE PIECES TO KEEP
GLOWING. I TRIED AND TRIED BUT NONE OF
THEM DID. AS SOON AS I SPAT THEM OUT, THEY
WERE ORDINARY GUM."

Her dream had snapped my mind crisply into focus and I
jittered with attention after she was done. I had so many different

thoughts, I felt that Other William might have found some way to hijack my head.

"I could look up Brian's accident," I said. "There'd be a report about the crash, an obituary listing a sister named Isobel. Once I find her, I can learn about you."

"THEY WEREN'T REAL NAMES," she said. "I DON'T REMEMBER HAVING A GIRLFRIEND OR BOYFRIEND OR ANYTHING IN HIGH SCHOOL."

"You said the dream was like a memory, though."

"IT WAS PROBABLY A FANTASY I HAD WHEN I WAS LONELY. OR A SHOW I SAW. OR MAYBE IT WAS TOTALLY A DREAM."

"How can you be sure?"

"DON'T YOU UNDERSTAND? IT'S THE PICTURE AND THE GUM. IT'S THE FLOWERS AT THE TREE. IT'S WANTING TO BE EIGHT-HUNDRED-AND-NINETY-TWO MILES AWAY, WHEN ALL I CAN DO IS STARE AT SOME MEMORY IN PLASTIC."

"I just want to know you more."

"I KNOW YOU DO," she said. "YOU ALWAYS WANT MORE. CAN'T IT BE ENOUGH SOMETIMES TO SHARE A DREAM?"

After the previous restless night and a half-day nap, I fell asleep early, woke in bed at 3 a.m., and stared at the pressed-tin ceiling.

June lay beside me. I rolled toward her and whispered her name. She didn't answer, and for a while I considered the nature of her sleep, which she'd told me was akin to a daydream or trance and was harder to disturb with physical sensation. I touched her with my palm, following her shape from her shoulder to her hip, and I wasn't fully sure if I had genuinely touched her or imagined I had felt her in my own drowsy trance.

My stomach still ached. When my thoughts kept turning to tapeworms and ulcers, I left June in bed, pulled a sweater over my undershirt, and walked to my study. I had already tidied the room after the catastrophic air spell, and the plastic sheets I'd used to cover the broken windows pulsed like lungs, in and out, and glowed softly amber from the streetlight below. Most of the pages I'd taped up for June had been torn away by the spell, and I spent half an hour covering the wall with the book's next chapters.

Something moved in my periphery. I turned and saw the ghostly couple from the kitchen standing near my reading chair. I watched them from my desk, thrilled to see another memory of their life and amazed—assuming they appeared at the same time every night—that I'd never before been awake in my study at 3:41 a.m.

As with their daily appearance in the kitchen, they looked like a movie projected onto mist. They were younger than before, as apple-cheeked as newlyweds. The wife's shoulder-length hair was wildly disheveled. She wore a diaphanous nightgown that both embarrassed and aroused me. The gown clung to her leg, drenched in blood from hip to hem. The husband stood beside her wearing boxer shorts and black socks. One of his socks had a suspender. He was muscular and lean, with chest hair in the shape of an upside-down triangle, but gave the impression of a child trying not to vomit. Only his chin and hands were bloody, as if he'd been splattered while he was dressed and then removed his shirt.

As far as I could tell, the blood wasn't theirs.

They stared together at the floor. There was a stain the size of a dinner plate that might have been blood but looked darker, like oil or ink. Something about the stain, especially its shape, transfixed me more than the couple and we all stared together, pondering its meaning.

The husband's legs wobbled. He knelt and sat back on his heels, his face a tightening knot that was painful to observe, and then he balled his hands and ground his whitened knuckles into his temples. He ground so hard, his eyes began to bulge. The wife pulled his hands away and said something firm. I couldn't hear her, but whatever she said caused the husband to drop his arms and sob.

He mumbled a reply. She slapped him on the cheek. Her violence seemed to shock him from his catatonic state and when he registered surprise, she slapped his other cheek.

More, I think he said.

She slapped him seventeen times until his face began to swell and then he looked at her, ecstatically and ferally alive.

The wife slumped and swayed. I thought she might faint until her husband stood and held her up, shaking her arms to rouse her. She recovered her balance, backed away, and offered him her cheek.

He slapped her face repeatedly, exactly as she'd done for him, and after thirteen slaps, the wife looked revitalized. They kissed each other then, passionate and bloody, and they almost seemed real until they vanished like steam.

I walked to where they'd stood and raised the corner of my rug, exposing the hardwood floor the couple had stared at half a century ago. The stain was there. I glanced away to pin the corner of the rug under my reading chair's foot, and when I looked back at the stain, the shape of it had changed.

I touched it with my finger, thinking it was wet. The stain

was perfectly dry and infused into the woodgrain, but whenever I glanced away, the shape of it would change.

I spent the next hour sitting in my chair, repeatedly averting my eyes and gazing at the stain, which altered its appearance in innumerable ways. Every shape it assumed was maddeningly familiar. I stared and stared, convinced at any moment I would glean its strange significance.

As soon as I turned my head, the answer flashed clear— it was an octopus, or my father's facial hair, or the abdominal scar of the girl to whom I'd lost my virginity—but then I would look and find the stain had morphed to something new, and resonantly true, and equally elusive.

"Maybe they killed someone," I said to June in the morning, after I'd told her about the couple's fresh appearance in the study. "They hurt each other to alleviate the guilt, and it worked so well, they turned it into a ritual."

"A PARENT OR A LOVER," June said. "OR A BABY."

"It might have been an accident."

We watched the stain throughout our conversation. It changed whenever we looked away, and even when we stared simultaneously, the shape appeared differently to each of us.

"Now it looks like Europe."

"I SEE A GIRAFFE."

"Look away and look back in three…two…one. Now I see an old woman with antlers."

"I SEE A BROKEN HEART, LIKE A CHEAP TATTOO."

We tried a more poetic approach to interpreting the stain, comparing its impressions to other intangible experiences.

"It's like staring at a distant tree moving in a breeze," I said, "when the leaves are like static with a weird, subliminal message."

"IT'S LIKE FORGETTING A PARTICULAR WORD FOR A PARTICULAR THING," June said, "AND EVERYONE YOU ASK FORGETS THE WORD, TOO."

"Tasting a faint but undeniable flavor in food."

"SEEING A MAN I NEVER MET BUT SWEAR I ONCE KISSED."

I knelt and touched the wood, feeling as if the answer was behind me, casting shadows.

"What did the couple see, though? Why did that part of their marriage leave a permanent impression?"

"THIS IS POINTLESS," June said. "LET'S TRY ANOTHER SPELL."

"I wonder what parts of our lives are that important. When somebody else owns this house a hundred years from now, will they see a spectral memory of us? What'll it be?"

"ME ALONE," June said. "YOU'LL BE DEAD AND I'LL BE HERE UNLESS WE FIND THE BOOK OF ELEMENTS."

I stood and rubbed my eyes, trying to divert my trancelike obsession, and walked toward my desk to get *The Spiral Grimoire*. The shape's hidden meaning was immediately clear.

"I've got it!" I said and turned around, solver of the riddle, only to find the shape had changed itself again.

I carried the grimoire and a milk crate full of supplies back to where I'd been and lingered for a moment, pondering the stain.

"YOU NEED TO FOCUS ON A SPELL NOW."

"I know, I know. Sorry."

I unrolled the study's rug to cover up the stain. The shape was in my head, though, shadowing my thoughts, and so I flipped through the spellbook and unpacked the crate to physically distract myself, matter over mind.

I'd gathered the required supplies from my own specimen collection and the oddments room, and after spreading them on the floor and staring at them a while, June examined the grimoire and said, "I DON'T UNDERSTAND THIS."

"It's more of a ritual than a spell."

"YOU'RE SUPPOSED TO BREATHE FIRE?"

"I think I'm supposed to speak it."

"HOW?"

"I'm not entirely sure."

The fire ritual's purpose was vague and most of the text was written in Old English, a language I barely understood. The rest of the page was illustrated with a series of crude pictograms, some of which indicated the necessary materials and preparations, others of which depicted a man astonishing witnesses with divine (or infernal) flame-words that jetted from his mouth.

I used a hammer to pulverize a block of sulfur and sprinkled the yellow powder into a symbol on the floor. The symbol was a three-foot diameter sun with rays shaped like tongues. The sulfur's eggy stench made my stomach loop and lurch, and my nausea deepened when I opened a jar of formaldehyde, used a pair of tongs, and dropped three red salamanders into the mortar I usually used for my breakfast banana.

"YOU HAD SALAMANDERS HANDY?" June asked.

"They're good for other things."

"I HAVE A STRANGE BOYFRIEND."

Her words preoccupied me enough to keep from gagging when I pulped the salamanders with the pestle, and I thought intently about the married couple in the kitchen when I slit my forearm with a knife and dribbled blood into the mash. I spooned a glob of the salamander-blood mixture onto each of the floor symbol's tongues and smeared the remainder in the middle as the grimoire instructed.

The final steps of the ritual were obscure. I stood inside the symbol, with my feet on the central mash, and tried reading portions of the Old English text. I raised my arms in a gesture similar to that of the fire-speaker's pictogram. I visualized flames in many shapes and forms, but when I imagined the resulting smoke, my thoughts drifted idly to the stain beneath the rug. Something about its change and permanence together hinted at an answer I was desperate to discover.

"ARE YOU SURE YOU'RE DOING IT RIGHT?" June asked.

"You shouldn't be standing in the circle."

"WHY NOT?"

"You might disrupt the elemental forces," I said. "Plus your questions are distracting."

"YOU ALREADY LOOK DISTRACTED. CONCENTRATE HARDER."

I changed the position of my arms, closed my eyes, and melodramatically creased my brow. June seemed to hover just outside the circle and I thought about the husband standing with his wife. They must have had ordinary, unbloodied lives when they weren't watching stains or cutting each other's arms. Had they celebrated holidays? Vacationed at the ocean? Had they told each other jokes and watched TV after dinner? I wondered how they'd looked completely undressed and if their tenderness or violence had carried into sex. Who had died first, and who had lost more: the one without life or the one without a partner?

"WILLIAM," June said.

"I'm trying."

"WHAT ARE YOU THINKING?"

"Fire, fire, fire."

"TAKE THIS SERIOUSLY," she said.

"Damn it, June, I am."

I walked out of the sulfur ring and crouched to ease a stomach cramp, wondering how she'd known my mind had started drifting.

"I KNOW, I'M SUCH A BRAT," she said.

"You're not a brat."

"ME ME ME."

"You're angry at me now?"

"WHY WOULD I BE ANGRY?"

"You're impossible to read. Tell me what you want."

"I WANT TO STOP FEELING LESS IMPORTANT THAN A STAIN."

I raised my knife-cut arm and said, "I'm bleeding for you, June. I'm skipping meals, grinding salamanders, trying to talk in fire. I barely leave your side so you'll never be alone. I'm trying to get the book."

"ARE YOU REALLY?" June said.

I dug my knuckles into my eyes until the pressure made colors. The stain was in my thoughts again, swirling and amorphous, and I didn't try to name it or the feelings I was feeling. She was wrong and she was right. I was trying and I wasn't. I kept my hands fisted so she couldn't touch my palms.

9. THERE ISN'T A SPELL FOR THIS

Nothing is more occult than someone else's heart.

We spent the day apart in wordless frustration that deepened into petulance. June drifted room to room, exploring the house and reading the new pages I'd taped to the study wall, and whenever we crossed paths, we went our separate ways as if we loved being lonely.

I leafed through books and puttered in the oddments room. I tried to reimagine Mr. Stick's garden, with its twilit sky and Polaroid trees, and wondered if my study didn't exist when it appeared or if the space was simultaneously two distinct places.

I tried to eat a tuna sandwich for lunch but couldn't swallow more than a few bites; either the sulfur and salamanders had poisoned my appetite, or my argument with June had filled me like cement.

Alone in my bedroom, I decided to boost my mood—and prove June wrong about my level of commitment—by opening *The Spiral Grimoire* and trying an Icelandic spell called the Hreinsar Regnstormur. According to lore, the spell produced a cloud that would cleanse anything from Viking longships to pestilent environments. A water spell, in other words: an element we needed. I followed the book's instructions, standing bare-chested and drawing interlocked runes in the air as I recited the translated verse:

Wound-worms and stains of swords
Flooded by the weather's words
Sea from sky upon us fall
Wash the blood and rinse the pall
With blades of rain is sorrow flensed
Grief and even death are cleansed

The poem continued for twenty more lines, and after three complete recitations, my bedroom's perpetual moisture started to condense where I had air-spelled the runes.

A miniature cloud formed. It was dark gray and the size of a marshmallow, hovering at the level of my chest and fulminating gently with purple electricity. Misty rain smudged the bottom of the cloud but the rain was too fine to ever reach the floor. I couldn't have washed my hands with such a miniscule storm, but I was proud of my success and believed, with care and practice, that subsequent attempts would yield a better cloud.

A tiny lightning bolt flickered like electrified hair. I leaned forward to examine the top of the storm, wondering if I would feel a breezy hint of updraft. The cloud abruptly moved and vanished into my chest.

My heartbeat skipped, shocked by the storm's concentrated voltage, and pressure under my sternum made it difficult to breathe. Pain streaked sharply through my shoulder and my jaw. I felt a mounting sense of doom and thought I might fall, and so I sat on the bed and closed my eyes, trying to settle my palpitations and wondering if I should run to the bathroom and chew a couple of aspirin.

The symptoms gradually faded but a heaviness remained. I felt as if a gallon of water—far more than the little cloud could possibly have held—had pooled above my diaphragm, weighing on my stomach. The atmosphere was heavy, too. A late-day gloom held me to the bed like a wet wool blanket covering my legs.

For the first time in months, I thought of my parents' bodies: the clothes they'd been buried in, their winter-cold bones, their coffins like fragile dark bubbles in the ground. It seemed as if a bubble around myself had also thinned, and when it burst, I'd be smothered and forgotten and alone.

June came into the bedroom. I sensed her at my side and wanted to soften things between us, but the day's long silence felt impenetrably dense and I might have lost hope, convinced we couldn't talk, if she hadn't reached out and written on my hand.

"DO YOU FEEL THAT?"

"What."

"LIKE SOMETHING WONDERFUL IS DYING."

It would have seemed maudlin if it didn't feel true, and not just true but tangibly external. The depression I was feeling went beyond me and June, and once she pointed it out, I felt an animating jolt. The spell's boggy weight stayed inside my body but I forced myself to rise, felt suddenly alert, and wondered what was causing such free-floating gloom.

"It's something in the house."

"UNDER US," she said.

I was hesitant to walk on my badly numbed feet, but then my circulation improved, my legs tingled warmly, and June and I left the bedroom and headed downstairs. We knew the way instinctively, following a woefulness as physical as mist, and found the source of our unease inside the first-floor utility room.

Dozens of house centipedes had swarmed around the doorway. They parted at my approach but not as nimbly as before, and I almost crushed a few of the laggards when I stepped toward the door. The utility room was dank and dark. Weak light from the adjoining room revealed the monstrous boiler with its grimy knobs and gauges. The centipede queen lay behind the boiler, motionless and pallid in the moldy wet corner. Her antennae were as slack as two damp ropes, and her large black eyes were lusterless and dry.

June had heard about the centipede but hadn't yet seen her, and she stood at my side and radiated warm fascination.

"SHE'S BEAUTIFUL."

"She is. But something's wrong with her," I said.

I stepped toward the queen, extending a hand as I had done on the night of our first encounter, but she didn't reach back or even twitch at my approach. I touched the top of her head and it was velvety and cold.

"It's me," I said. "It's William."

One of her antennae half-lifted in response, reminding me of a wounded dog trying to wag its tail.

"IS SHE HURT?" June said.

"I don't know. Maybe she's sick."

I squeezed between the boiler and the queen's languid body, careful not to step on any of her limbs. The boiler was just shy of scalding and its rusty, greased surface scraped my bare back.

"I'm going to lift you," I told the queen.

I curled my arms under her segmented trunk and strained to pick her up. She was at least a hundred pounds of dull, saggy weight, and the water spell had left me feeling aqueous and weak. My left knee crackled and my back nearly seized but I was able to clear the boiler and stand up straight.

June wrote on my neck. "TWO OF HER LEGS FELL OFF."

I craned around and saw the legs quivering on the floor.

"It's an involuntary defense mechanism," I said. "She's stressed. It's nothing personal. Her legs will grow back, like a sea-star's arms."

I carried her upstairs to my bedroom and laid her on the bed before my strength gave out. When I knelt and tried looking into her huge black eyes, the window to her centipedal soul felt closed. I hoped my soothing tone would communicate care.

"You're safe. You're not alone," I said. "We'll help however we can."

I asked if she was hungry, wriggling fingers near my mouth to indicate spiders. I took a cup of water from my nightstand, poured a little in my palm, and offered her a drink. She watched me unresponsively.

"There must be some medicine or nutrient. A spell in one of my books."

"THERE ISN'T A SPELL FOR THIS," June said.

"For what?"

"IT'S LIKE AN EVIL LITTLE COAL SMOLDERING INSIDE HER. NO LIGHT. NO SMOKE. NO REASON IT SHOULD BE THERE. IT'S FILLING HER WITH POISON FUMES NOBODY CAN SEE. CAN'T YOU FEEL IT?" June asked. "HAVEN'T YOU FELT THIS BEFORE?"

"I don't know. I've been lonely. I've been sad for no reason."

"IT'S NOT THE SAME THING."

"I've grieved."

"THAT'S NOT THE SAME, EITHER."

My thoughts had the feeling of an outstretched hand, unable to reach another hand withdrawing in the dark. I knew what June was saying but the revelation hid her; she was someone I could trace but couldn't truly plumb.

"There's got to be something we can do."

"SHE NEEDS A BLANKET," June said.

I rummaged through my closet for a spare quilt, draped it over the queen, and tucked it under her legs as gently as I could. Her brood of tiny centipedes had followed up the stairs. They crawled on top of the quilt and settled on their mother. I helped a few of the stragglers up and stood back, admiring the cozy tableau, but somehow the coziness was even more dejecting. She was a prodigy of nature swaddled in warmth and safety, but she seemed beyond reach and didn't seem to care.

"I don't understand what's happening," I said.

"WE DON'T NEED TO UNDERSTAND IT. WE ONLY NEED TO STAY WITH HER."

Before we settled in, I went to my study for an entertaining book of insect legends, and then to the curiosities closet for a jar of live spiders in case the queen decided to eat.

When I opened the closet, I was surprised to see the Hungarian curler—the insect I'd saved after Mr. Gormly's booby trap—hovering in its Mason jar. The curler was still in the cocoon it had fashioned from my hair, but the cocoon itself floated and appeared to gently shake as if the pupa was imbued with a strong static energy. I touched the side of the jar. The hair cocoon wiggled, seemingly attracted to my own electric charge.

Curious as I was, I put it from my mind. I took the spiders for the queen and shut the closet door. When I made it back to my bedroom, I lit an eggnog candle, quietly played the radio, and sat with June at the side of the bed. I read some stories to the queen, but although her children waggled their antennae at my voice, she herself seemed dead and I eventually lost heart and put the book aside.

My absorption of the thundercloud continued to afflict me. The quaggy weight in my chest had spread throughout my body. Everything from my eyelids to my fingertips felt sodden, and my thoughts had the pruniness of over-soaked toes.

The radio signal faded and we listened to the static while I petted the queen's head. She made a centipede-shaped depression in the mattress.

"YOU HAVEN'T TALKED ABOUT YOUR MOM SINCE WE MET MR. STICK," June said.

I sighed and felt a deeper sigh hiding in my lungs.

"He answered mysteries with mysteries."

"YOU LEARNED SHE USED THE BOOK."

"I learned I wasn't enough. I always blamed some accident or force for what happened. Now I know she left me and my father, came here whenever she could, and used the book because she wanted something more than what she had."

"YOU CAME HERE, TOO."

"Only because of her."

"YOU WERE OBSESSED WITH ALL HER STORIES EVEN BEFORE YOU LOST HER."

"I was a kid. I was excited."

"YOU WERE JUST LIKE HER. NOBODY'S HAPPY WITH THE HERE AND NOW, AT LEAST NOT FOR LONG. LOOK AT THE CENTIPEDE, DEPRESSED WITH ALL HER KIDDIES ON HER BACK."

"You think we're doomed to be unhappy?"

"WE'RE IDIOTS WITH HOLES. BUT JUST BECAUSE A PERSON NEEDS SOMETHING MORE DOESN'T MEAN THEY DON'T LOVE EVERYTHING THEY HAVE. YOU SAID IT ABOUT YOURSELF," she said. "YOU FELL IN LOVE WITH REACHING."

"What hurts is that my mom hasn't reached back."

I watched the little centipedes clinging to their mother and my eyelashes sagged like rows of antennae.

"HOW DID SHE FINALLY DIE?" June asked.

I told her about the night I'd gotten out of bed and found her in the living room. I told her about the rising parallelogram of light, the vision of her ghost doubling her body, and the depthless, empty darkness of her pupils when she faded.

"I don't remember anything that happened after that," I said. "Apparently I fell and hit my head against the baseboard. Eventually my father woke up and came to the living room, found me unconscious and my mother dead, and called 911. My memory of the next few hours didn't stick. It was almost like my own life flickered when she died.

"I'd never known the world without my mom in it, so after she was gone, everything was different. I couldn't tell her about anything anymore. Whatever I did or felt was emptier and lonelier. There was motherless rain, motherless grass. Motherless pizza. Motherless bedtime. I looked all the time, praying for an inkling. I thought if I could glimpse an afterplace she'd gone to—if that world was there, maybe she was, too."

Nothing in the room, including myself, felt solid.

"My dad didn't think we'd see my mom again. To him, death was death and nothing happened afterward. The whole work of life was holding onto life. But then he swerved to save a deer, crashed his car, and died, so I really don't know what he actually believed. Maybe he was right about holding onto life—that even as a ghost, nothing's more important."

"WOULD YOU SWERVE TO SAVE A DEER?"

"Maybe. I don't know."

"WOULD YOU RISK YOURSELF FOR ME?"

"That's a whole different thing."

"WHAT IF THE RISK WASN'T DEATH BUT SOMETHING SAD YOU HAD TO LIVE WITH?"

June touched my temple. It might have been a kiss. My head felt stuffed with warm, swelling sponges, and just before the pressure in my skull became unbearable, two plump tears dribbled from my eyes. The tears wet my cheeks and quivered under my chin. I huddled on the floor and slobbered into my hands. My thoughts blurred away and I was purely, fully sad— sad without memory or worry or regret, sad without beginning or end, absolutely sad.

I cried a long time, unembarrassed by the phlegm bubbling from my nostrils and the coughing sounds, weirdly like laughter, of my sobs. The muscles in my face were tighter than a fist. June rubbed my arm until the outpour mellowed.

My body slumped and ached. I saw the queen and all her children, blurry on the bed, and when I turned toward June, the space where she invisibly sat was faintly luminescent from the lamplight glancing off the moisture of my lashes.

I wiped my nose along my shoulder and my eyes kept drizzling.

"YOU OK?" June said.

"I'm still crying."

"YOU MUST HAVE MORE TO CRY ABOUT."

I wondered if the queen's strange affliction was affecting me, or maybe…

"It's the spell," I said.

"WHAT SPELL?"

"It was meant for cleaning bloody ships, plague houses— whatever needed rinsing. I made a miniature thunderstorm, like something that would float above a cartoon character's head.

The storm went into my chest. I think it's coming out now."

"YOU'RE CRYING RAIN?"

I sniffed and wiped my cheeks, unsure of whether the spell or something else was coming out of me.

"The grimoire didn't say how to stop it."

"DON'T TRY TO STOP IT. IT'LL END WHEN IT'S DONE."

"What if it doesn't?"

"IT WILL."

"How do you know that?"

"THAT'S HOW CRYING WORKS," she said. "HONESTLY, WILLIAM. YOU'RE ONE OF THE MOST WARMBLOODED PEOPLE I'VE EVER MET, BUT SOMETIMES YOU TALK LIKE YOU'VE NEVER HAD A BODY."

Sensing June was right didn't lessen my discomfort. In fact, it only spurred me to attempt, with stoic will, to regulate a process out of my control.

I'd read of monks who could slow their hearts to five beats per minute, mystics who could levitate, and shamans who could mentally move a tumor from a patient's body into a nearby gourd that was suitable for burning.

Surely, if I tried, I could stop my own tears.

But since I didn't want June to see me try and maybe fail, I dabbed my eyes with a facecloth and pretended I was content to let my crying run its course. We stayed with the centipede queen and her brood, discussing everything but my tears, until I had to replace the soaked facecloth with a towel and June finally said, "WE DON'T HAVE TO TALK ABOUT YOUR CRYING, BUT NOT TALKING ABOUT IT WON'T

MAKE IT STOP."

"I'm not *not* talking about it," I said. "I'm letting it happen like you said."

"IF YOU WANT TO KEEP DISTRACTING YOURSELF, THAT'S OK, TOO. THERE'S NO WRONG WAY TO CRY."

My ability to visualize her expressions had grown in recent days, and now whatever I did or said with regard to my crying produced the same result on June's imagined face: the look of a mother, sad and patient, letting a child make mistakes.

"I need a drink," I said.

"OK."

"I'll be back."

"I'LL BE HERE."

I left June and the centipedes and went to the downstairs bathroom, where I took an antihistamine and sat on the closed toilet, allowing myself to cry more openly in private in the hope that I would get it out and purge myself completely.

I rinsed my face with cold water to soothe my puffy lids, and then I lay on the cool linoleum floor with a cloth draped across my eyes. When the antihistamines didn't help after an hour, I went to my study and researched counterspells, incantations, and desiccant boluses, but reading was almost impossible because of the constant blur and dampened pages.

I tried to sleep but tears rolled down my temples when I reclined in my chair, tickling me and pooling in the porches of my ears. Still I drifted for a while, halfway out of consciousness, and daydreamed my head was sinking in a bog. My hair, the chair's headrest, and my shirt were chilled and damp. My heart was swampy, too, and although I'd assumed the spell was primarily to blame, my tears began to sadden me and feed their own flow, the way an artificial laugh can trigger real amusement.

Cheerful music, ice packs, and calisthenics failed. I checked in with June and tried to feign interest when she told me the queen had raised her antennae.

"SHE SENSED YOU COMING BACK," she said. "IT SEEMED TO PERK HER UP."

But the queen looked as crumpled and despairing as before, and my only qualm about leaving the bedroom again was that June would think, correctly, that all I really cared about was lessening my tears.

My cheeks and lips burned. My eyes were pickled eggs. Over the next few hours, I drank a dozen cups of water to prevent dehydration but was drained, wrung, and crying as if I'd dribble into nothing.

I took a shower, hoping the body-wide rinse would distract me from my plight, only to feel as if my tears had gathered reinforcement. I wrapped my head in a towel until the weight became unbearable, and when I took the towel off, my head was heavier than ever.

Just before dawn, I abandoned hope and slumped back to my study, where I sat and stared at the floor and let the tears fall. A puddle formed, big enough to patter with my feet. I thought about my life, as crying people do, and wondered what wellspring of suffering was in me. It was more than losing my parents or the threat of losing June. Everything, including me, seemed to be dissolvable.

The sun rose gray behind thick winter mist. I crossed the room, leaving footprints on the floorboards with tear-wet soles, and tore the plastic sheet off one of the broken windows. The outside air was unusually warm, and the swirling mist around the parked cars, brownstones, and distant church steeple had a springtime freshness that reminded me of crocuses. Snowpack remained but something deep had changed. Icicles dripped. The mist soothed my face and then a breeze, much warmer than the already pleasant air, swept back my hair and I inhaled, breathing hard, until it felt as if the gust had blown straight through me.

My body felt rinsed from the inside out. I wasn't crying anymore, and it suddenly seemed incredible that I'd spent the night in tears—that the sky had been so dark, I'd believed the world was melting, and I'd suffered by myself instead of curling into June.

I reattached the window plastic with a staple gun and dawn-lit vigor. Awake, relieved, and cleansed, I was eager to see June and the centipede queen and headed for the bedroom. My only ache was gastric, which I at first attributed to hunger, and yet the pain was less an emptiness and more a stabbing bloat, as if the storm I'd absorbed had hardened in my stomach and its lightning bolts had turned into tiny, jabbing fulgurites. I wondered again if I'd inhaled a shard of glass during the air-summoning spell, but I had seen no evidence of internal bleeding, and so I swigged some Pepto-Bismol, massaged my aching gut, and went upstairs, hoping the discomfort would diminish.

The little centipedes had scattered from their mother's back and greeted me with perky activity, scurrying to and fro, up the walls and onto the ceiling. I walked across the room and smiled at the queen, who had climbed off the bed and eaten the spiders I'd brought her the previous night. Her eyes had grown soulful and alive instead of vacant, and she nuzzled against my leg, almost knocking me off-balance when I rubbed the top of her head.

I turned toward June, sensing her on the floor exactly where I'd left her.

"You were right," I said. "My crying ran its course. I feel OK."

And yet I suddenly had the feeling I was talking to myself, as if she weren't really there quite as I'd imagined. I saw myself objectively, surrounded by centipedes and talking to an invisible friend, and wondered how I ever took a bit of it for granted.

"I'm sorry I left you here alone."

I reached out my upturned palm for June to answer.

"Hey," I said. "I'm back. Everything's all right now. There's an amazing warm breeze outside. I'm going to open some of the windows and air the place out. We can walk together and talk."

"I HELD HER ANTENNAE," June finally said.

"That's good. She must have liked that."

"I FELT WHAT SHE WAS FEELING. I REMEMBERED BEING A KID, PULLING LEGS OFF A CRICKET AND WONDERING WHAT IT FELT. WHAT ITS INSECT BRAIN KNEW OR UNDERSTOOD. I FELT IT WITH THE QUEEN WHEN I TOUCHED HER ANTENNAE."

"What did it feel like?"

"FAMILIAR. LIKE A THING I'D ALWAYS KNOWN AND SPENT MY LIFE PRETENDING…"

"What?"

"I DON'T KNOW. I DON'T FEEL VERY…"

"June," I said. "I'm here with you. Tell me what's the matter."

"I HELD HER ANTENNAE AND WE MADE A KIND OF CIRCUIT. I DREW THE FEELING OUT OF HER AND GAVE HER SOME OF ME. SHE GOT BETTER. I GOT WORSE."

I wanted to hold and reassure her, but all I could do was softly sway my hands through her space. She seemed to pull away from me without really moving.

"If you could exchange energy with the queen, you can do it with me, too," I said. "Lean into me and let me share whatever you absorbed."

"IT ISN'T LIKE THAT WITH US."

"It is," I said. "It could be. Keep talking to me now. That's a circuit, too."

"I NEED TO BE ALONE."

"Don't disappear. It isn't good for you. It worries me."

"I WON'T DISAPPEAR," she said. "WALK ME TO THE ROOM WITH THE WEIRD LITTLE TREE."

"Why?"

She didn't answer but she stood. I could tell by the angle of her hand when she touched me, leading me to stand with her and follow her out of the bedroom. The centipedes watched us go. Before we walked away, I turned to look at the queen, hoping her energy would help, but all I felt was June's silent desperation.

We reached the end of the hall and started downstairs.

"What are you going to do?" I asked.

"SIT," June said.

"Let me bring a lamp. I'll get the radio for you, too."

"I NEED THE DARK AND QUIET. JUST MYSELF FOR A WHILE."

"You shouldn't be alone if you're feeling this bad."

June stopped walking halfway down the stairs, in the shadowy space where neither story's light was able to reach. I turned and gripped the handrail, creaking on a step, and raised my hand toward her in the manner of a suitor.

"I'M SCARED OF BEING ALONE," she said.

"That's why I ought to stay with you."

"WHEN I WAS LITTLE, I HAD NIGHT TERRORS

ABOUT ETERNITY. THEY WERE HALF-CONSCIOUS NIGHTMARES, LIKE REALLY VIVID FEVER DREAMS. I'D WALK AROUND THE HOUSE AND TELL MY PARENTS WHAT I WAS DREAMING. I EVEN MADE SUGGESTIONS, LIKE MAYBE TURNING ON THE TV WOULD FULLY WAKE ME UP. BUT NOTHING EVER WORKED."

"What did you dream about?" I said.

"I WAS TERRIFIED OF NUMBERS. ESPECIALLY THE NUMBER NINE. I NEVER UNDERSTOOD WHY, BUT BEING SCARED OF SOMETHING THAT MEANT NOTHING MADE IT SCARIER SOMEHOW. AND THEN I DREAMED I WAS SMALL AND SPACE FELT DISTORTED. MY MOTHER WOULD HOLD ME BUT HER FACE LOOKED A HUNDRED FEET AWAY. I'D IMAGINE I WAS ALONE, A TRILLION LIGHTYEARS AWAY AND FLOATING IN THE DARK, IN A PLACE BETWEEN STARS WHERE I COULDN'T SEE THEM FLICKER. I WAS THAT FAR OUT. EVEN STARLIGHT COULDN'T REACH ME. AND NOBODY WOULD COME AND THERE WAS NO WAY HOME."

"How'd you make it stop?"

"I DON'T KNOW. I JUST WOKE UP," she said. "BUT NOW I CAN'T WAKE UP AND I'M ALONE AND OUT OF REACH."

"You're not alone. I'm not going anywhere."

"DO YOU KNOW WHAT I THOUGHT ABOUT LAST NIGHT, HOLDING THE QUEEN'S ANTENNAE? BEING HERE IN THE HOUSE FOR YEARS. FOR DECADES. AND MAYBE I'LL FIND SOME PEACE WITH OUR LIFE HERE TOGETHER. BUT THEN

EVENTUALLY YOU'LL DIE AND I'LL BE HERE WITH NO ONE TO TALK TO, AND NOBODY ELSE WILL SEE ME, AND I'LL STAY THAT WAY FOREVER."

Years, I thought. Decades. Our life here together.

She passed me on the stairs and said, "I NEED YOU TO OPEN THE ROOM FOR ME."

I followed her down to the first floor, into the dining room, and past the table from which I'd once collected the luminous indoor snow. The room was cold and glumly brown, more like a root cellar than a place to sit and eat, and the door at the opposite end she needed me to open seemed an entryway to someplace earthier and deeper.

We hadn't revisited the room since discovering the sapling growing from the wall. I wondered if the tree had died without light, but before I could open the door to see, June's hand covered my own on the knob.

"LET ME IN. THEN CLOSE THE DOOR."

"You'll be trapped."

"THAT'S THE POINT."

"Why are you doing this?" I asked.

"WHENEVER I'VE DISAPPEARED, WHENEVER I'VE COME BACK, IT'S HAPPENED ON ITS OWN. I NEED TO DO IT ON PURPOSE AND HAUNT MYSELF A WHILE. PROMISE NOT TO COME AND LET ME OUT. NO MATTER WHAT."

"I don't like this."

"I KNOW."

She took her hand off mine.

I slowly turned the knob and opened the door just enough to let her slip past. I was unable—or afraid—to look inside the room and see the darkness she was craving.

I almost said a thing but didn't, worried it would cast a spell that scared her even more. Certain words are dangerous to anyone who says them. They can ricochet, or meet a force they can't overcome, and cut their way back like bits of swallowed glass.

I waited half a minute once she passed through the gap, and when I shut the door behind her and the gap disappeared, I felt as if I'd literally closed her into nothing.

10. THE THING IN MY GUT

I wandered through the house, restless and eager to talk with nothing to do and no one to talk to. The queen and her children were gone when I returned to the bedroom. How a hundred-pound centipede could hide herself so easily was beyond my understanding, but I found no trace of her as I wandered through the house.

I lingered in the room where I'd met Other William. My craving for conversation notwithstanding, I sensed that neither of us wanted to engage that morning—that we were sick of ourselves, and therefore of each other—and we went our separate but identical ways in our identical, separate brownstones.

Downstairs I passed the basement door and pressed my ear to the wood, listening in vain for Mr. Gormly's radio and wishing, yet again, we could establish some rapport. I made my way to the kitchen where my stomach, unnaturally bloated and tender, could barely tolerate coffee, let alone breakfast. I had missed the married couple's daily appearance in the kitchen and wondered if they—mere vestiges of life—were sentient enough to ever feel lonely.

The house was dead, top to bottom. I went to my study with habitual steps, as unaware of my progression as someone who rises in the night, urinates in the bathroom, and returns to bed without forming a memory of doing so. I found myself standing in the center of the room, staring idly at my shelves of closed, quiet books. My thoughts were like a needle on a record's locked groove, crackling and perpetual, fuzz upon fuzz.

"Hello," I said, mostly just to hear my own voice.

I remembered doing the same the day I moved in. The day I met June.

"Hello," I said again.

It was a satisfying word, benevolent and hopeful. It was an opening. A window.

"Hello," I said. "Hellooo."

I closed my eyes, imagining the word flying forward like a flashlight beam lancing into space—a sound made of light connecting me to someone. I felt a warm color growing in my chest as if I'd swallowed something nourishing and fabulous and hot.

I took a strong breath and bellowed out, "Hello!"

Yellow-white fire jetted from my mouth.

I gasped, jumped back, and clamped my jaw shut in surprise. I felt a crunch underfoot and saw that I'd trampled a mound of sulfur and pulped salamander. Standing in the sun-shaped circle on the floor, I had somehow finally made the fire spell work.

I exhaled and said, "Whoa."

The word was mint green, freshening the study's drab brick walls. After trying to calm my pulse and quiet my mind, I focused on the fire moving in my throat. My larynx was a combustion chamber. My epiglottis fluttered from the updraft heat. The flames didn't burn my esophagus or tongue, and once I grew accustomed to the pilot-light sensation in my voice box, I experimented with various words and marveled at the colors flashing from my mouth.

"Firelight," was orange.

"Look," was royal blue.

"Beautiful" was luscious pink and "powerful" was violet.

The word "sky," repeated a dozen times, changed hues as I envisioned different weather and seasons. I spoke my name and saw a spectrum, as familiar and mysterious as looking in a mirror. Everything I said, however dull, became miraculous. I sounded like a blowtorch ejaculating feelings. All my life I'd associated certain words with colors, but to now produce the effect gave me a surge of otherworldly vigor, and I thought of people watching me and listening with rapture. I would awe Mr. Gormly. I would spellbind June.

But although my body was impervious to the flames, surrounding objects weren't. A sneeze charred my curtains. The study's temperature rose dramatically, a houseplant wilted, and the ceiling paint blistered and began to bubble off.

Soon the word-colors changed. The flames grew dirtier and I exhaled a foul, oily smoke that stung my eyes and hazed the room. My breathing became increasingly labored as I gasped the smoky air and expressed myself in frustrated tones.

I leaped out of the symbol on the floor to no avail. A gulp of coffee turned to steam and flash-burned my knuckles. My uncontrollable coughs scorched the corner of my desk and incinerated a stack of penciled notes—my own voice destroying what I'd written.

I ran to the window for a breath of fresh air. Before I reached the sill, I saw the three-winged pigeon through the plastic over the sash.

"Oh!" I blurted out.

The crimson word flashed directly at the sheet and melting plastic fell on the pigeon, smothering its flaps and efforts to escape. I grabbed the blob off the sill before it tumbled down to the street, burned my hands, bobbled it, and dropped it on the floor. The pigeon jerked and crinkled, trapped inside the plastic and making a distress call that sounded, literally, like a bird being cooked to death in overheated shrink wrap.

I tried to tear it free but the congealing plastic glued to its feathers. I'd have ripped the pigeon apart before I got it out. Instead of letting it suffocate and suffer any longer, I steeled myself and whacked its little head against the windowsill. The pigeon fell still and softened in the plastic.

I yelled a scarlet sound. Tears sizzled on my face. Faint from lack of oxygen, I concentrated hard on opposites of fire and shouted them into the room, hoping to break the spell.

"Water! Cold! Ice!"

Fiery, every one.

"Dark! Winter! Death!"

They were smoke, soot, and ash. Then I thought the word "snow" and had a pristine hope.

I ran from the poisonous study downstairs to the curiosities closet, where I hacked a ball of flame and almost set the door ablaze. There in the closet, in a Mason jar nestled on a shelf, was the melted luminous snow I'd collected from the dining room.

I unscrewed the cap and gulped half the liquid. The water soothed my windpipe with cool, cleansing vapor that reminded me of guzzling cold soda as a child. I hacked a glob of tar that dribbled down my chin and coughed until my lungs filled with air instead of smoke. An inrush of oxygen tingled through my body.

Still I felt as if I'd eaten wads of wet cigarettes. I put the snow jar down and prostrated myself on the floor, convinced I was going to be sick, but as soon as I started gagging, my abdominal muscles contracted so painfully that I fought the urge to vomit and rolled onto my back.

My shirt was undamaged from the fire I'd been breathing, but when I yanked it up and exposed my midriff, it was as swollen and red as if I'd doused myself with boiling water. I was aghast to see my bellybutton—an outie since birth—had turned into a dark, puckered hole. The edges of the hole were angrily enflamed.

Despite the blazing sting, I very slowly probed it. My entire index finger fit inside my navel, the lining of which had grown peculiarly firm, and my fingertip encountered something solid in my gut.

I palpated my abdomen and determined, with tears streaming out of my tightly closed eyes, that the mystery object wasn't a shard of glass or anything I'd eaten. It had the edges and the angles of a small, hard box. Its corners jabbed inflexibly whenever I tried to sit, and I needed several minutes to stand and hobble to the bathroom.

I was sweating grotesquely despite a deep inner chill, and after rinsing my face and finding a thermometer, I found I was running a reverse fever of 95.1 Fahrenheit. My stomach alone felt hot, as if the object inside me was absorbing all my heat. I drank half a bottle of Pepto-Bismol and examined my puckered navel more closely in the mirror, but then a whiff of smoke alarmed me and I returned to my study, afraid my fiery breath had left something smoldering.

Walking back was agony, as each step shifted the mystery object in my gut, but I finally reached the study and was relieved to see only a lingering haze hanging in the room. Nothing had kept burning and little of true value had been irredeemably damaged... nothing but the pigeon lying on the floor, snap-necked and welded into the blob of melted plastic.

I sobbed again, hurting my stomach with convulsions, and when I crossed the room and knelt beside the pigeon, its tiny eye, exposed through a gap in the plastic, reminded me of my mother's eyes the instant she had died.

I laid my hands over its wings.

"I'm sorry," I said. "I'm sorry."

Something dug into the corner of my knee, and when I shifted my leg, I saw the pigeon's key lying on the floor. I picked it up and discovered it was, in fact, made of bone. It was four inches long, unnaturally cold, and resembled a fish rib with three human teeth growing off one end. The teeth were two incisors and a molar.

I squeezed the key in my fist and slumped down sideways. The open window's air cascaded over my body and I rolled onto my back, closed my eyes, and fell asleep beside the pigeon with the mystery object heavy in my stomach and the bone key's teeth biting into my palm.

I woke up shivering to dull, plunging pain and a metallic chill spread throughout my body. It was as if whatever was in my stomach were an unmeltable block of ice with my essential heat—my warmer self—frozen in its core.

A fresh look at the pigeon made my torment feel deserved, and yet I couldn't bear the pain. I had to get it out. I examined my navel, the mouth of which had puffed and reddened like an acid burn. I pressed the object through my distended belly and was able to rotate it slightly so one of the corners jutted upward into the bottom of my navel cavity.

I had a peculiar feeling of accomplishment, as if I'd reached the final hour of a pregnancy that had, despite its wrongness, grown something special and remarkable inside me. Suddenly, instinctively, I knew exactly what to do.

After an awkward fight to stand, I walked downstairs, locked myself in the bathroom, and sterilized the pigeon's bone key with rubbing alcohol. I undressed, climbed into the empty bathtub, and doused my belly with iodine. My navel fizzed and bubbled.

I swallowed a jigger of St. Madelia's spirits to numb the pain without clouding my senses. My fear was strong but vague. I had little knowledge of umbilical extraction, aside from obscure references to the autovivisectionist cult of 14th-century Florence, and I had no way of knowing if my solution would be successful or fatal.

I pressed the key into my navel. When it was three inches deep and couldn't be inserted any farther, I held my breath and turned the key clockwise. Something popped like a packing bubble breaking underwater. The key's teeth found purchase and I felt a bizarre abdominal twist, as if my vitals were spaghetti winding around a fork.

After one full turn, the key lodged tight and wouldn't move in either direction. I was sweating profusely and was queasy from the iodine smell, and the sight of a bone protruding from my stomach was almost too horrid to endure. I considered giving up and calling 911, but my aversion to hospitals—and the unlikelihood that anyone there could help—redoubled my commitment.

I took a slow breath, squeezed the key, and tugged.

The mystery object rose inside my stomach as if it had bonded to the key. My navel stretched open to accommodate its passage. There was a hideous sound of suction, like a plunger being yanked out of deep, thick mud, and although my swig of St. Madelia's spirits alleviated most of the physical pain, there was no avoiding the psychological trauma of pulling a solid, four-inch cuboid out of my bellybutton.

I feared that when the object fully emerged, my insides would geyser from the dilated hole, and I paused before the final tug, regretting numerous choices in my life and wishing I had, in some way, expressed myself more meaningfully to June before she'd left again.

The key and the object slurped free in a splutter of pink-white goo. My navel snapped shut as neatly as a rubber seal. From relief or mounting shock, I lost consciousness for an undetermined time and had a hallucinatory dream of turning inside-out.

When I came to my senses, the box and key were lying separately near my sternum, and my navel—though swollen and weeping fluid—was once again the neatly tied outie of my birth.

I was ravenously hungry. After a quick cold rinse, I toweled off and walked to the kitchen with such single-minded voracity, I temporarily forgot about the mystery object I had left unexamined in the tub. I guzzled orange juice straight from the bottle, started a pot of coffee, fried half a dozen eggs with shredded cheese, and buttered four slices of toast. I wolfed the eggs and toast standing at the table, and when I was done I felt so energized and new, I jumped straight up and high-fived the ceiling like a teenager showing off just because he could. I hadn't realized how drained I'd gradually come to feel over the previous days, and I vowed to be more positive and light moving forward.

My optimism vanished with the last bite of egg. I drank my coffee and thought of June, sitting without me in the dark, and of the three-winged pigeon I had recklessly destroyed. My memories of the centipede queen, my night of crying, my fiery words, and finally my navel flashed kaleidoscopically.

The thing I'd grown. *The object*. What the hell was it?

I returned to the bathroom, walking calmly as my thoughts raced eagerly ahead, preparing me to comprehend whatever I'd discover there.

It lay in the porcelain tub, rinsed of its umbilical goo but coated with a gray, gelatinous substance that made it slippery to hold. I held it under the faucet and scraped the gel away with my fingernails, revealing a solid rectangular object that was three inches wide, four inches long, and as thick as my thumb.

The surface was two flat plates of pale, flawless bone. The plates were joined along one of the vertical edges by a flexible hinge, like a bivalve's ligaments, which allowed me to open them and reveal a profusion of membranous sheets within. The sheets were impossibly thin—there must have been hundreds of individual layers—but they were supple and unrippable. Each of them had a distinct pattern of red and violet symbols, like capillaries forming strange calligraphy in skin.

I closed the pages in the covers.

"My God," I said. "The book."

11. MY OWN SHADOW

"I never did an earth spell," I said to Other William. "Only air, water, and fire."

"I didn't need to summon earth," he said.

The insight occurred to me simultaneously and I nodded at its rightness. The book's skin and bone were my skin and bone. My own live flesh had been the element of earth.

Other William and I sat in our identical chairs, in our respective rooms, each of us holding a copy of *The Book of Elements* open in our laps. We'd spent hours alone that day, paging through the book and trying to decipher its mysterious language, but the writing had proved as alluringly difficult to read as the lines of our own palms. At times epiphany seemed near, and the capillary symbols would appear to course with blood, but then the meaning would dissolve beneath the superficial patterns.

"Mom was able to read it," I said. "So was Mr. Stick."

"Maybe the book knows I didn't really want it to appear."

"I wanted this so much, I tugged it out of my guts."

"And part of me regrets it," Other William said. "Now I have to choose exactly how I'll use it. Maybe the book can't be read until my *thoughts* are comprehensible."

"I want to help June. How's that for comprehensible?"

"Don't ignore the rest," Other William said. "I want to help June, but I don't want to lose her. She'll be gone and out of reach,

165

exactly like Mom."

I thought of June in the dark and couldn't visualize the scene. Had the tree growing out of the wall budded and flourished, or had it died from lack of light and turned to brittle wood? What if she'd changed her mind about retreating into solitude? She might have spent hours pawing at the door, calling to me without sound and tearlessly crying, or vanished into a deeper dark beyond my understanding. All I knew was she had chosen to go and hadn't yet returned.

"If I use the book to help her," Other William said, "it'll be just like this. I'll be here, on my own, having to guess if she's OK, except there won't be a chance of her ever coming back. But there's another way to play it."

"I don't understand."

"I could try to find Mom."

"Assuming it's even possible the book can find Mom," I said, "what would be the point? Of course I'd love to be with her and talk with her some more, but I can't resurrect her. I'd have to let her go again. And how could I begin explaining that to June? That I had the book and used it for myself instead of her."

"Mr. Stick said the book disappears after use. June will never know once the evidence is gone. Talk to Mom, keep June—it's a win-win."

I experienced a version of the room spinning around me, but it felt as if my mind and not the walls had started twirling. My thoughts spiraled off, independent of my brain, and for the first time since meeting Other William, I began to lose sense of which of us was speaking.

"I can't betray June. I promised her I'd help."

"There are other ways to help."

"I'll hate myself."

"I'll live with it."

"She'll suffer."

"She'll be loved."

"I'm needy and I'm selfish."

"So is she."

"So was Mom."

We stood and knocked our chairs back, each of us leaning forward with our copy of the book and dangerously close to nosing past the threshold. Other William's face was sickly and misshapen, like heavy lard molded into a likeness of myself, and he was either too grotesquely false or far too real. I wanted to mash his head and squeeze the grease through my fingers.

"You don't love her if you trap her."

"You don't love her if you let her go."

"She doesn't love *you*," we both said at once.

We dropped our books and lunged. Our arms crossed the doorway, and as soon as we seized each other's throats, the earlier spinning intensified and the house, the world, and everything I knew revolved around my body. My thoughts sprang forward into Other William's eyes. Looking out and looking in with equal concentration, my doppelganger's otherness was suddenly a sameness and I couldn't tell which of us was genuinely me.

We backed away.

My consciousness was briefly counterclockwise. Astonishment and fear unbloomed and disappeared. I felt as if I hadn't yet lunged at Other William, and our estrangement slowly grew until it seemed we'd never met before. The room felt altered in a way I couldn't pinpoint. I wondered if we'd spun and swapped places in the scuffle.

I knelt and picked up my book. So did Other William.

When we closed the doors, we locked each other in instead

of out, and it was hard to tell which of us was thinking in my head.

Unsure of how long *The Book of Elements* would remain in its current state, I sealed it into a Pyrex food container with a snap-lock lid, hoping that if it decomposed into a less stable element, I might prevent its essence from immediately dispersing.

I left the container in the fridge and dove into busywork—washing dishes, folding laundry, sweeping the sulfur and mashed salamander off the study floor—to distract myself from the corkscrewing questions in my mind.

I resealed the study's broken window with a fresh sheet of plastic. I examined everything I'd scorched with my incendiary words, repairing what I could and disposing of anything unsalvageable, and lit a boysenberry candle to mask the stink of burnt paint.

I went to the oddments room, gathered several items into a milk crate, and returned to the study, where I placed the dead pigeon on top of the supplies and carried everything up to the brownstone's roof. The day's early gentleness had chilled to wintry cold again. Freezing mist gathered in my hair and made the rooftop dangerously slick, and after gazing at the red sunset, I put the crate down and knelt, working carefully but quickly with the items I'd collected.

I tied strings to the four corners of a broad handkerchief, then tied the dangling ends to a deflated balloon. After laying the pigeon on the open handkerchief, I ignited a mercury seed inside the balloon. The seed began to burn and heat the inner air.

I cradled the pigeon's body—it was soft and nearly weightless—until the balloon had fully inflated.

"I'm sorry," I said, and raised my palms.

The balloon sailed gently northwest above the city, floating in the dusk and glowing from within. I watched until the pigeon drifted over the domed roof of the city's music hall, and then a breeze swept it upward and it vanished in the fog.

I mussed the frozen moisture off my hair, picked up the milk crate, and skidded my way back to the stairs, where I descended into the darkness of the house and closed the roof hatch above me.

I slouched down to my bedroom, prepared for a night of insomnia, and had barely flicked the light on when June rushed toward me.

She hugged me like a staticky blanket and said, "WHERE WERE YOU? I CHECKED EVERY ROOM. WE MUST HAVE ORBITED EACH OTHER ON THE FRONT AND BACK STAIRS."

"You're back," I said. "Thank God. I've been worried—"

"SO HAVE I! I SAW THE DAMAGE IN THE STUDY AND THOUGHT YOU MIGHT HAVE COMBUSTED, TRYING TO SUMMON FIRE. TELL ME YOU'RE OK. WHAT HAPPENED? ARE YOU HURT?"

"It's been a really hard day. I need to lie down."

We went together to the bed, walking-drifting with our hands invisibly enlaced, and I unbuttoned my shirt and stripped down to my tee, exposing the length of my arm for June to touch and trace on. I almost took my T-shirt off, too, but my itchy navel reminded me I hadn't fully healed and something in me puckered up tightly and inverted.

I told her about the fire spell's unexpected force and how I'd accidentally killed the three-winged pigeon. I swore I heard her gasp, like suction in my head, but then she listened and found the story so vivid and amazing, from the first fiery word to the quenching drink of snow, that she me double back and tell the whole thing again.

"I'M SORRY I WASN'T HERE."

"What did you do in there alone? How did you open the door?"

"I FOUND ANOTHER WAY OUT. I'LL TELL YOU ALL ABOUT IT BUT THERE'S SOMETHING MORE IMPORTANT FIRST."

"What?"

"IT CRUSHED ME THAT THE CENTIPEDE GOT BETTER OVERNIGHT."

"What do you mean? I thought you liked her."

"I DO," June said. "I THOUGHT I UNDERSTOOD HER. HOW WEIRD IS THAT? THE FIRST TIME IN MONTHS I MEET A KINDRED SPIRIT AND IT'S A HUNDRED-POUND BUG."

"You and I are kindred spirits."

"YOU AND I SHARE A LIGHT. I THOUGHT THE CENTIPEDE AND I SHARED SOMETHING ELSE. BUT WE DIDN'T AND IT MADE ME FEEL A THOUSAND TIMES WORSE. A SINGLE NIGHT AND SHE WAS BETTER. UP AND AT 'EM, EATING SPIDERS. SO I JUST DECIDED FUCK IT. I'LL *CHOOSE* TO BE ALONE."

"June," I said.

"WAIT. I NEED TO TELL YOU HOW I DIED."

"I'VE ALWAYS FELT LIKE MY OWN SHADOW. LIKE A BRAVER, SUNNIER ME WAS WALKING OUT FRONT AND I WAS CAST BEHIND, DRAGGING ON THE GROUND.

"I'D WAKE IN THE MORNING FROM THESE HOLLOWED-OUT DREAMS. LIKE BLEACHED-OUT PICTURES OF SOMEONE ELSE'S MEMORIES. THE DREAMS WOULD CARRY OVER INTO MY DAY. I COULDN'T SHAKE THEM. EVERYTHING WAS MEMORIES I DIDN'T WANT TO HAVE.

"IT DIDN'T MAKE SENSE. I NEVER UNDERSTOOD IT. I FELT LIKE I BELONGED SOMEWHERE ELSE. MAYBE NOWHERE. ONE DAY I STARTED TO WONDER HOW IT WOULD BE IF I WAS GONE, AND ONCE I SAID IT TO MYSELF, IT WAS THERE. IT WAS REAL.

"I STARTED EXPERIMENTING, SEEING HOW MANY DAYS I COULD GO WITHOUT A REAL CONVERSATION. HOW LONG IT WOULD TAKE A FRIEND TO NOTICE I HADN'T TEXTED. HOW LONG I COULD SIT IN A CAFÉ BEFORE ANYBODY MADE EYE CONTACT.

"ONE NIGHT IN DECEMBER, I WALKED AROUND DOWNTOWN. IT WAS A FRIDAY. SHOPS AND BARS WERE OPEN. PLENTY OF PEOPLE ON THE STREET. I DIDN'T GET ONE HELLO. NOT A NOD, NOT A GLANCE. NOT A SINGLE CREEPY GUY LEERING WHEN I PASSED.

"IT WAS LATE AND COLD AND I WALKED TO THE BRIDGE OVER THE RIVER. I STOPPED HALFWAY ACROSS, ON THE WALK BETWEEN THE ROAD AND THE SAFETY RAIL, AND I CLIMBED UP AND SAT ON THE RAIL WITH BOTH LEGS DANGLING OVER. I LEANED TOWARD THE WATER WITH MY HAIR AROUND MY CHEEKS.

"THIRTY-SEVEN CARS DROVE PAST. THIRTY-SEVEN! NOBODY BEEPED OR STOPPED. NOBODY NOTICED ME AT ALL. I WAS PROBABLY SHADOWED SOMEHOW, OUT OF SIGHT IN SOME WAY. BUT I'D SPENT THE NIGHT PROVING NOBODY COULD SEE ME, SO I DIDN'T FEEL HIDDEN. I ONLY FELT UNSEEABLE.

"THE RIVER HAD MOSTLY FROZEN. IT WAS JIGSAW ICE, SOLID AT THE BANKS BUT SHIFTING UNDER THE BRIDGE, AND EVEN IN THE DARK, I SAW THE PIECES MOVING. THERE WERE CRACKS. THERE WERE BREAKS. THERE WAS ONE BLACK GAP DIRECTLY UNDERNEATH ME AND I THOUGHT, THAT'S FOR ME. THAT'S WHERE I BELONG.

"I DON'T REMEMBER JUMPING. ONLY FALLING OFF THE BRIDGE.

"I LANDED IN THE GAP BUT MY ELBOWS HIT THE ICE. EVERYTHING EXPLODED. TOTAL DARK. TOTAL COLD. INCREDIBLE SHOCK AND PAIN AND TOTAL FUCKING PANIC. I COULDN'T MOVE MY ARMS SO I KICKED AGAINST THE CURRENT, AND I DIDN'T KNOW WHICH WAY WAS UP UNTIL MY BACK BUMPED THE ICE.

"I WAS TRAPPED UNDERWATER AND THERE WASN'T ANY LIGHT. NO WAY TO FIND AN OPENING EXCEPT BY FEEL. I WANTED IT TO END. I ALMOST JUST QUIT AND LET MYSELF SINK.

"BUT THEN MY FACE BOBBED UP THROUGH A FISSURE IN THE ICE. I COUGHED AND GASPED, AND I MANAGED TO SLING ONE OF MY ARMS ONTO THE SURFACE AND HOLD MYSELF UP.

"THE STARS WERE SO CLEAR, I WASN'T SURE IF THEY WERE REAL. I WAS DRIFTING PAST RIVERFRONT PARK AND SAW THE BUS STOP A HUNDRED YARDS AWAY. THERE WAS A WOMAN WITH A BRIGHT RED HAT. I SAW THE WINDOW OF THE BOOKSTORE I'D BROWSED AN HOUR EARLIER, AND IT WAS ALL SO STRANGE, REMEMBERING I'D BEEN THERE, STANDING IN THE CITY, AND SUDDENLY THE WORLD WAS FARAWAY AND MAKE-BELIEVE. LIKE A HOLIDAY SCENE WITH MINI FIGURINES AND PERFECT LITTLE TREES AND TINY CUPS OF COCOA.

"MY ARM SLIPPED. I SANK AGAIN. BEFORE I COULD POP BACK UP, THE ICE DRIFTED OVER ME AND TRAPPED ME UNDERNEATH. I KICKED AND FLAILED, AND BUMPED MY HEAD, AND EVERYTHING WAS OUT OF REACH JUST ABOVE THE ICE. AIR AND LIGHT AND PEOPLE.

"I HAD THIS VISION OF CIDER DONUTS BACK IN MY APARTMENT. I SWEAR TO GOD, I WAS DROWNING AND POOF: I SAW THE DONUTS. AND I THOUGHT OF HOW I COULD EAT THE WHOLE BAG OF DONUTS, AND WATCH SCI-FI MOVIES ALL NIGHT, AND GET DRUNK, AND FUCK SOMEBODY, AND QUIT MY JOB, AND DRIVE WHEREVER I WANTED UNTIL MY CAR DIED, AND IF I GOT FAT AND DEPRESSED AND LONELY AND LOST IN THE MIDDLE OF NOWHERE, ALL OF THAT WAS BETTER THAN DROWNING IN THE DARK.

"AND THEN SOMETHING HAPPENED. I DON'T KNOW HOW TO DESCRIBE EXACTLY HOW IT FELT.

IT'S LIKE THE THING YOUR MOM TOLD YOU. WE CHOOSE A WAY FORWARD.

"THERE WAS A QUESTION BUT THE WORDS WEREN'T ORDINARY WORDS. THEY WERE IMPOSSIBLE TO TRANSLATE BUT STRONG AND UNDERSTANDABLE. THE QUESTION WAS FAMILIAR. I'D ANSWERED IT BEFORE I WAS BORN AND SOMEHOW, EVERY DAY OF MY LIFE, I'D BEEN CONSTANTLY AWARE OF MY ANSWER WITHOUT REALIZING IT.

"THE QUESTION WASN'T LIVE OR DIE, EXIST OR DON'T EXIST. IT WAS MORE LIKE YES OR NO. AND WHEN I FELT IT UNDERWATER, I CHOSE THEM BOTH TOGETHER. NO AND YES. YES AND NO.

"MY BODY SANK AWAY FROM ME. I STOPPED FEELING ANYTHING PHYSICAL LIKE COLD, OR SUFFOCATION, OR THE PAIN OF MY BROKEN ARMS. THE ONLY THING I FELT WAS ME, DIVIDED FROM MY BODY, AND NOTHING IN MY LIFE HAD EVER FELT LONELIER.

"I GUESS I WAS A GHOST THEN. AT FIRST I STAYED IN THE RIVER, MOVING WITH THE CURRENT, AND THEN I WAS OVER THE ICE AND EVERYTHING WAS WHITE AND GRAY. I KEPT FLICKERING OUT AND REAPPEARING SOMEWHERE ELSE, AND ALL I REMEMBER ARE THE FLASHES WHEN I FLICKERED BACK ON. I HEARD POLICE SIRENS, THEN NOTHING. I SAW THE INSIDE OF A CHIMNEY, AND A CELLAR, AND A BEDROOM FULL OF FERNS. I APPEARED INSIDE

THE BODY OF A LITTLE GIRL AND SCARED HER SO BAD, SHE PUKED INTO HER BATH. THEN THERE WAS NOTHING FOR A WHILE. FOR A LONG, LONG TIME.

"EVENTUALLY I WAS HERE, BUT EVEN HERE I FLICKERED OUT. THERE WAS NOTHING. I WAS NOTHING. EVERYTHING WAS GONE. I DIDN'T SEE OR THINK OR FEEL ANYTHING AT ALL UNTIL I SENSED YOU IN THE BEDROOM THE DAY YOU MOVED IN.

"YESTERDAY IN THE ROOM, AFTER YOU LOCKED ME IN, THE DARK CLOSED AROUND ME AND THE ROOM BEGAN TO CHANGE. THE TREE WAS DEAD AND TWISTED. THE CEILING SAGGED TOWARD ME. IT FELT LIKE THE WHOLE HOUSE WAS BURIED UNDERGROUND.

"I TOLD YOU ABOUT THE NIGHT TERRORS I HAD WHEN I WAS A KID. MY MOTHER USED TO SAY I OUGHT TO MOVE AROUND THE FEAR, EXPLORING IT AND FEELING IT. MAKING IT FAMILIAR. SO INSTEAD OF FADING OUT OR TRYING TO LEAVE THE ROOM, I JUST SAT THERE, SURROUNDED BY THE DEAD TREE'S BRANCHES. I DIDN'T TRY TO FEEL HAPPIER OR SAFER. I LET MYSELF BE SAD AND TOALLY ALONE. AND AFTER HOURS OF ACCEPTING IT AND BEING WHO I WAS, I JUST THOUGHT OF COMING BACK AND BEING HERE WITH YOU.

"AND SUDDENLY HERE I WAS AGAIN, STANDING IN THE HOUSE. I WALKED AROUND AND LOOKED FOR YOU AND DIDN'T FEEL SCARED. AND THEN I

FOUND YOU IN YOUR ROOM AND HERE WE ARE. BACK TOGETHER."

I felt as if the room had disappeared while she talked—as if her story had been happening and I had been a ghost, moving through her past, from the river to the house, and we'd finally reached the present, just as we had left it, and my body and my room had materialized again. I saw the door frame's crooked rosettes, the hair on my forearm, and the wrinkly faded pumpkin on my bed's patchwork quilt. I heard the children's choir of the radiator pipes and caught a whiff of dust drifting through my sinuses.

"DID YOU GET ALL THAT?" she asked.

I slowly found my voice, like something I'd misplaced.

"I've never been suicidal but I think I understand."

"THE WORDS, THOUGH," she said. "YOU UNDERSTOOD THE WORDS?"

My eyebrows frowned.

"I WASN'T WRITING IN YOUR HAND."

"What do you mean?"

"I WAS TALKING AND YOU HEARD ME. I'M DOING IT RIGHT NOW."

I stared at my naked arm, astonished to feel her hand resting on my skin and knowing it had been there, motionless and soft, throughout the telling of her story. I wasn't reading words written on my body. I simply comprehended everything she said.

"It isn't ordinary sound," I said, contrasting it to the bed creaks and the physical vibrations of my own spoken voice. "How are you doing this?"

"THE SAME WAY I TALKED TO MR. STICK. I'M THINKING ALL MY WORDS AT YOU AND SUDDENLY YOU HEAR THEM. CAN YOU SEE ME

NOW, TOO?"

I stared into the space where she was sitting at my side but couldn't see a trace of June's silhouette.

"No," I said. "Nothing. But God, I really hear you! Say something else."

"I SLIT THE SHEET THE SHEET I SLIT AND ON THE SLITTED SHEET I SIT."

"Wow."

"I HAVE NO TONGUE TO TWIST."

"I even hear the *tone* of your voice. What happens when you sing?"

"ROW, ROW, ROW YOUR BOAT GENTLY DOWN THE STREAM. MERRILY, MERRILY, MERRILY, MERRILY, LIFE IS BUT A DREAM."

"I heard that," I said. "I might have tricked myself, though. The words and melody have always gone together in my head. Sing the same words to a different common song. If I recognize the melody, we'll know I'm really hearing it."

Her laugh—I heard her laugh—was fruity and contagious.

"THIS IS HARD," she said. "OK. I'VE GOT ONE. HERE IT GOES...

ROW ROW ROW YOUR BOAT
GENTLY DOWN THE STREAM.
MERRILY-MERRILY-MERRILY-MERRILY,
LIFE IS BUT A DREAM."

"That was 'Twinkle, Twinkle, Little Star!"
"RIGHT."
"It worked, I really heard you. But wait wait wait. I'm sorry."
"WHY?"

"Everything you said about your life, about your death—we should talk about that."

"I ALREADY DID," June said. "I WANTED YOU TO KNOW AND NOW YOU KNOW. IT'S WHAT I NEEDED. COME ON, I'VE GOT TO SHOW YOU SOMETHING."

"What?"

"YOU'RE GONNA LOVE IT."

12. THE UNDERHOUSE

At June's urging, I took a rain-scented candle and a matchbook off my nightstand, and then she led me by the hand up the hallway, downstairs to the first floor, and through the dining room to the door where we had stood, only a day ago, before she went inside and made me lock her in.

"Here?" I asked.

"HERE."

I gripped the knob again, experiencing an awful déjà vu, as if the two of us were doomed to endless separation.

"We're going in together, right?"

"YES," June said.

I opened the door and felt a rush of warm, loamy air. June caressed my arm, encouraging me to step inside and close the door behind us, and once the dark was absolute, I squatted to put the candle on the floor and struck a match. The wick caught, the candle's glass jar began glowing, and I stood and walked forward with the light raised before me.

I immediately stopped, astonished by a bewildering maze of flickering limbs and shadows. The fragile little sapling growing sideways out of the wall had burgeoned into a tree that filled the whole room. I stepped forward and a leafy bough pressed against my chest. Another brushed my hair. Others hemmed my legs.

I held the candle up and out, illuminating the trunk and

the enormous splayed roots that gripped the wall like a claw. Downward-growing limbs supported the tree's horizontal weight, and the profusion of other branches radiated to the ceiling and the corners of the room. Moon-white bark sheathed the trunk and branches, and the floorboards were undulant with spongy green moss.

The tree's abundant leaves were delicately orange. Small, milky blossoms tipped every sprig. The petals winked and fluttered, like the eyelids of lovers, and miniature bees bobbed around the flowers. I was stung several times but the pain was oddly pleasant, reminding me of sunlight prickling on skin.

June and I moved to the base of the trunk, she in her sinuous ghostly way—I pictured her as mist drifting through the gaps— and I in a stumbling hunch, butting my shoulders on the branches. The tree's array of shadows bent and wobbled in the candlelight, and even once we reached the trunk and I balanced the candle on a cushiony mushroom, the wavering flame made everything around us pulse and breathe.

We sat a long time on the moss, touching hands and drowsing to the bees' buzzy hum. I recognized a smell I'd forgotten since my childhood—a Creamsicle, garden-hose, sweaty-palm fragrance that was dreamier than daydreams and plusher than nostalgia.

Having finally heard June's voice, I was satisfied with silence. I wondered what senses were essential to connection. How much of what I loved ever had a body? How much of it was memory, and hope, and other ghosts?

"I'm hungry," I said.

I'd fallen asleep. The candle looked noticeably shorter and my voice sounded oddly disembodied in the quiet. Habit opened

my hand for June to write an answer and I was thrilled again—
even more somehow—when I simply heard her say:

"I BARELY REMEMBER MY STOMACH
GROWLING. I USUALLY ATE BEFORE I WAS HUNGRY,
WHENEVER I WAS SAD OR BORED. I LOVED IT SO
MUCH. IT WAS SUCH A SIMPLE FIX. I MISS HOW
EASY IT WAS TO INSTANTLY FEEL BETTER WITH
A CRUMB CAKE."

She had the graveled, dusky tone of private conversations
and I was peacefully aroused, as if we'd just had sex and I could
feel her silky weight without needing more.

"GO EMOTIONALLY EAT FOR ME," she said.

"I'm actually hungry."

"SAVOR IT AND TELL ME ALL ABOUT IT WHEN
YOU'RE DONE."

"Come to the kitchen with me."

"I'LL STAY FOR NOW," she said. "TAKE THE
CANDLE WHEN YOU GO. I DON'T MIND THE DARK
NOW."

I caressed her leg and wondered again how much of my
perception—the faint electric tingle when I touched her, my
visualization of her thigh and knee—was only in my head. My
stomach churned and gibbered. I stood with the candle and
bumped my head on a branch. A bee stung my ear as I made my
way to the door, which I propped slightly open with a chair in
case June changed her mind and decided to follow me out.

"Right back," I said.

She answered with a sleepy-headed, satisfied, "HMMM."

I blew out the candle, went to the kitchen, and poured a cup
of scorched coffee from the pot I'd forgotten to turn off many
hours earlier. Fluffy snow fell from lavender-gray clouds and

melted on the window. It was twilight—five-thirty, according to the wall clock—but I couldn't remember if it was A.M. or P.M.

When I opened the refrigerator, my hunger turned to nausea. I reached between the orange juice and eggs and lifted out the Pyrex container, and then I closed the fridge and pulled a chair away from the table. The chair's rubber feet stuttered across the linoleum. I sat with the cold glass container on my lap, opened the snap-lock lid, and laid my hand firmly on the cover of the book.

After hours in the fridge it was still at body temperature, having lost none of its heat—my heat, I supposed, from when it had grown inside my stomach. The cover was smooth, flawless bone, and the ultrathin pages were as velvety as the inside of my cheek. I sat for five or ten minutes, afraid to open the book in case the strange arterial writing made itself legible.

I had an Etch A Sketch once, years before my mother died. I kept it in my room, on the dresser near my bed, and for a few weeks after I got it, I'd sketch something new before I fell asleep. Every morning, I'd wake up and find my mother had answered with a little sketched smiley face, a heart, or maybe a word. She denied it for a while, just to keep me guessing. I loved leaving sketches, knowing they'd be answered, but the novelty wore off and one night I stopped. I didn't stop on purpose. I forgot and that was it. I couldn't even remember the last thing we sketched, and eventually I shook the board clear and it was done.

Now all I had to do was open the book and use it, and whether or not I found my mom, I'd always have June. I'd never have to live without contact again.

"THAT'S THE CREEPIEST SANDWICH I'VE EVER SEEN."

I jumped at June's voice and tried to clap the lid back onto the Pyrex. Instead I dropped the container and it shattered at my feet, skittering fragments over the floor and exposing the book completely. I snatched a dish towel off the sink and rushed to cover the book.

It opened on its own before I had a chance. The cover parted like an oyster shell, the pages fluttered and settled, and although the writing remained obscure, the symbols flowed and slithered into mesmerizing shapes.

"WHOOOA, WHAT IS THAT?"

"June—"

"IS THAT THE *BOOK?*"

Her tone was bright and buoyant: a melody on the rise. I clutched the towel and backed against the sink, unable to think of anything to say that didn't feel like broken glass crunching under my shoes.

"MY GOD, YOU REALLY GOT IT. DID YOU TRY A NEW SPELL OR WAS IT ALL OF THEM TOGETHER?"

"I grew it in my stomach…"

"HOLY SHIT, FOR REAL? NO WONDER YOU HAD CRAMPS. SO THE SPELLS WERE WORKING THE WHOLE TIME AND WE DIDN'T EVEN REALIZE. BUT WAIT-WAIT-WAIT. HOW'D YOU GET IT *OUT* OF YOUR STOMACH? DO I EVEN WANT TO KNOW?"

I leaned forward and gripped the chair-back for balance, unable to lift my head and feeling heavy enough to drive the chair's legs through the floor.

"I found the pigeon's key after he was dead."

I told her everything in monotone: my worsening abdominal pain, my navel as a keyhole, climbing into the bathtub, and pulling out the book. She held my hand atop the chair-back and stood close beside me, but in the pause that followed my story, all of her retracted. Her hand left my hand. Her air left my air.

"THIS DIDN'T JUST APPEAR NOW," she said, stating a fact so obvious, it pained me to know how many minutes she'd managed to convince herself otherwise.

"I didn't know how to tell you."

"JUNE, I HAVE THE BOOK."

"It wasn't that easy."

"I DON'T KNOW WHAT YOU'RE SAYING."

"Don't you understand? I thought I came here to find my mom or maybe find answers, but mostly I was sick of feeling haunted by myself. Then I met you and didn't feel haunted."

"I COULD HAVE BEEN ANYBODY, THEN."

"But you weren't. You were you."

"YOU USED ME," June said.

"You used me, too. Help me, William. Get the book. Let me disappear. Didn't you ever think it might be hard for me, too?"

"SO YOU LIED."

"I didn't lie. I needed time to think."

"I TOLD YOU EVERYTHING," she said. "EVERYTHING BAD ABOUT MYSELF."

"There's nothing bad."

"THERE IS TO ME. I HATED MYSELF AND DROWNED MYSELF AND NOW IT'S LIKE I'M PERMANENTLY TRAPPED UNDER ICE. AT LEAST I HAD YOU."

"You *do* have me. You told me everything you hate about yourself. I loved you *more*."

"BUT NOT ENOUGH TO HELP ME."

"I don't want to lose you."

Underneath my voice was Other William's voice, an echo that was shadowing and muddying my words, except I felt as if my honesty was panicking and paining him, forcing him to say what would drive June away.

"I FINALLY THOUGHT SOMEBODY COULD SEE ME," June said. "INSTEAD I'M A GHOST YOU INVENTED. I'M AN IMAGINARY GIRL. ALL YOU EVER SAW WAS WHAT WAS IN YOUR HEAD."

I didn't know where she'd gone and swayed my hand through the air as if the room had gone dark and I was feeling for a light.

"DON'T TOUCH ME," June said. "DON'T EVEN TRY TO REACH ME."

"I'm sorry, I shouldn't have hidden it."

"GO ON AND KEEP THE BOOK. I DON'T WANT ANYTHING ANYMORE."

"June," I said. "Come back to me. You're spiraling again."

"I'M SICK OF BEING ALIVE AND SCARED OF BEING DEAD AND NONE OF THAT'LL CHANGE WHETHER I'M HERE OR SOMEWHERE ELSE. IT'S EASIER AND BETTER IF I REALLY DISAPPEAR."

I walked across the kitchen, pulverizing glass, until my fingertips found her in the doorway space.

"Stay with me. I'm sorry. I was selfish, I was scared."

"NONE OF THIS WAS REAL," June said, and then she vanished.

Instead of trying to find her in the house, I went for help.

I picked *The Book of Elements* out of the glass, carried it up to my study, and placed it on my desk underneath a paperweight. Margarine light warmed the air—it was morning, I discovered— and I sat in my reading chair, closed my eyes, and concentrated hard to visualize the room.

I pictured the brick and mortar walls, the century-old

floorboards, the mysterious shifting bloodstain, the scorched furniture and ceiling, the plastic-sheeted windows, and most of all the bookcases, which I extended wider and deeper in my imagination until they stretched beyond the room, surrounding me completely. Books upon books and pages after pages, as dense and never-ending as a primeval forest.

When I opened my eyes, my familiar study remained unchanged, and so I tried again, much longer this time, until I couldn't feel my body and my thoughts, free to float, alarmed me with their dizzying, self-sustaining motion. Something loosened in my head. It wasn't a release of ordinary tension, but rather as if my consciousness had always been a knot and I was pulling on the end and steadily unraveling it.

My last sober thought was that I was sleep-deprived and desperate. Then I felt as if I'd turned into a panoply of pages—an efflorescing book, blooming other books. My spine, my guts, my atoms, and my senses whirled apart. I was a story rearranging into endless different stories with a million starts and finishes and living, shifting middles.

I opened up my eyes, unsure my eyes were real.

Everything consisted of the pages I imagined. The walls were books instead of bricks, mortared tight with pulp, and the floorboards were hardcover spines packed together. My chairs and desk were paper mâché that hadn't yet hardened. They contorted and reformed themselves in gluey, strange distortions. My actual books were swarming words, like colonies of ants, and the floor lamp radiated signals and ideas.

I stood in the center, looking out and looking in from every vantage point—from the lamp, the bricks, the floor, and every wriggling letter. I watched myself watching how I watched myself watch.

I opened my eyes, confused because I'd opened them already, and the study had returned to its brick-and-oak state. My books were normal books, the furniture was firm. I sat in my chair and thought, "My mind is clear and sharp," just as anybody sane or crazy might have done.

I looked across the room and Mr. Stick sat at my desk, a naked old man of pale, shrively smoke. I didn't know if I'd summoned him out of his garden into my room or if my consciousness had reached into the plane where he existed. Either way, he didn't notice I was with him.

He studied what appeared to be an astronomy atlas, the pages of which were black with gently drifting stars. I walked across the room, stood at his side, and placed a finger on his book. Stars moved around my touch, as if my fingertip had gravity, and magnified their light by gathering together.

Mr. Stick reared back, startled by the change.

He looked around the room but I was invisible to him, and so he focused on the book with spellbound absorption.

I wrote, "Hello, Mr. Stick," by swirling the stars' positions, intuitively, into new constellations that accorded with my thoughts.

He answered in his voiceless way, contorting his face and body into elegant, flowing language.

Hello, he said. *Who are you?*

I constellated my name.

William! Is it you? I dreamed of this and doubted it. I might be dreaming now but what's the difference after all? How are you writing in my book?

"With my finger."

With your finger! What a gas. I'm a ghost being haunted by a man. Unless you're dead. You haven't died, I hope.

"No."

I'm glad to hear it. The house feels stronger with a dash of flowing blood. But how do you even see me?

"Please, I need your help. June's disappeared."

She's a Christmas light, he said. *She's bound to blink and flicker.*

"It's different this time. She told me how she died."

She was a suicide, or halfway so. I knew as soon as I met her. She's an equinox soul and always was, darling girl.

"She's trying to kill herself again. I need to find her right away."

If she isn't in the house, she's likely in the underhouse.

"The one with Other William?"

That's another house, he said. *I assumed Mr. Gormly had told you about the underhouse.*

"I've never even seen Mr. Gormly."

I never saw him, either. We talked via notes. He's a solitary walnut, impossible to crack, but as reliable and duty-bound as anyone I've known. I view him as a colleague—a watcher at a threshold.

"What threshold?"

The basement floor between the houses, Mr. Stick said. *The underhouse is structurally identical to this house—brick to brick, room to room—but wholly underground. God knows who built it, let alone why. Houses have psyches, as you already know, and the underhouse's psyche is malevolent. Deranged. Whenever there's a breach and some of its influence escapes, Mr. Gormly seals it up. I have little notion how. The man's entire existence is occult, even to occultists such as you and I.*

I thought of the stifling, dark miasma that had left me unconscious—the basement smoke I'd thought Mr. Gormly had released. He'd been trying to contain it. The little fiend had saved me.

"Why would June be in the underhouse?"

I thought you understood. It's where she goes whenever she vanishes.

"How?"

I sank there only once, after your mother wandered off and didn't come back. I was a newborn ghost. I'd expected and embraced a solitary life, but the actual experience was bluer than I'd dreamed. A mountaintop monk, however faithful to his calling, is bound to panic now and then when the silence, and the night, and the permanence surrounds him. I pitied myself. I missed my old connections to the world. And then I sank, against my will, directly into the underhouse.

Imagine going home and everything is dead. Imagine falling asleep and waking in a corpse. The underhouse convinces you you'll feel that way forever. I cozied into hopelessness and darkened into gloom. Living is difficult, you know, and there's a terrible seduction to the thought of nonexistence. I fear I would have let myself fade… if not for luck.

A young couple sneaked into the empty house one night and, to phrase it graciously, began to youngly couple. I sensed them from the underhouse, just as June, I suspect, later sensed you. I felt a hint of curiosity, as if the faintest possible breath had stirred me out of sleep—a breath I didn't care about and wasn't sure was real.

I followed my curiosity, reappeared here in the house, and saw the couple on the floor. Apparently I manifested in some way because they saw me and fled—she wearing only a skirt, he wearing only a T-shirt and sneakers—and their naked fear was so spirited and lovely, I was aroused back to life. I was charmed back to being.

"I could lure June back."

Not if she's surrendered.

"If the underhouse is physical, there must be some way in."

Mr. Gormly's iron safe functions like a ship hatch—a passage with a door. Sometimes he unlocks the safe to vent the atmosphere. I know what you're suggesting, but your body won't survive. Even for a ghost, the underhouse is lethal. It simply takes longer for a spirit to dissolve.

"You could go again," I said. "You could bring her back."

Mr. Stick condensed as if the temperature had plunged. His fluent shape froze; he seemed incapable of answering. I wrote more boldly in his book of constellations, moving stars as if my finger were a strong black hole.

"She's lost without your help."

I can't, he said. *I'll fail. Anyone can vanish—plenty of people do—but it takes rare fire to repeatedly appear. I don't have that fire.*

"June does."

Yes. She willed herself to linger as a ghost when she died. But if she's choosing to dissolve now, there's no way to help. The underhouse would kill you before you even found her.

"Only if I'm alive."

He coiled like smoke over a burned-out log that had caught a swish of air and was about to reignite.

"Can I make myself a ghost without *The Book of Elements?*"

It's commoner than you know, Mr. Stick said. *Most people linger several minutes after death. The trick will be enduring many minutes longer. You'll have to want to live and die intensely, simultaneously.*

"I will," I said. "I have to."

Dying is the easy part.

"Tell me what to do."

13. MY ELABORATE DEATH

Mr. Stick gave advice, I improvised a plan, and my stubborn desperation turned to reckless hope. I thanked him for his help and left him to his reading, and by the time I finished writing a note to Mr. Gormly—a crucial first step—Mr. Stick's vaporous form had faded from the study.

I took the note to Mr. Gormly downstairs and entered the basement with my pocketlight in front of me, relieved to find the air was only ordinarily musty. For now, the subterranean danger was contained. But the basement seemed darker than usual, confining my light to a compact sphere beyond which everything was totally benighted. I paid extra attention to the hardwood planks and iron plates that covered much of the damp, earthen floor—presumably Mr. Gormly's ad hoc repairs to underhouse breaches—and I imagined with dreadful fascination the evil twin house existing underfoot.

I came to the basement's northeast corner, where Mr. Gormly's massive black safe faced me from his barricade of junk and broken furniture. Most of the safe was covered but its door remained exposed. I raised my light and found a gap in the barricade's complexity, and into the gap I slipped the note I'd written in the study.

Dear Mr. Gormly,

I require immediate entry into the underhouse. A life depends on it. Please help.

Sincerely,
William

I'd barely deposited the note and lowered my pocketlight when a mint-scented envelope whizzed from the barricade and tapped me on the temple. I picked it off the floor and read Mr. Gormly's impossibly quick reply.

Foolhardy.
Combination 31L 7R 19¾L.
Bring centipedes. Leave burial instructions.

Sincerely,
Mr. Gormly

"The centipedes. Of course," I thought, grateful he had offered such practical advice.

Having failed to bring a pen to write another note, I answered him by speaking directly into the gap.

"I need to go upstairs and make preparations. When I come back down, I won't be able to move the dial and handle. I'll need you to open the safe for me."

The barricade didn't creak, no additional envelope issued from within, and Mr. Gormly's silence almost nullified what little goodwill he'd earned moments earlier.

"If you won't come out and help," I said, "I'll have to open it now."

I challenged his resolve by kneeling at the safe and dialing the combination. Thirty-one left, seven right... my defiance lost some its power when I failed to precisely dial nineteen-and-three-quarters left and I was forced to try again, six more times, before the safe unlocked.

"I'm opening it," I said. "You leave me no other choice."

I cranked the handle down and paused, staring at the barricade and waiting for him to clatter out, panicked and contrite, before I opened the portal and flooded the basement with the underhouse's baleful atmosphere.

Mr. Gormly called my bluff and there was nothing I could do. I'd figure something out. He'd done enough. I didn't need him.

I left the safe unlocked but closed and told him, "I'll be back in one hour. Don't relock it while I'm gone."

I returned to the main house, closed the basement door behind me, and banged a hand truck and empty milk crates up to the oddments room, where I rummaged through the boxes and utility racks for anything I could use to execute my plan.

After carting my gathered materials downstairs and unloading them in the bathroom, I carried a cassette recorder up to my study. I placed the recorder on my desk, located an obscure leather-bound manuscript in my bookcase, and flipped it open to a ritual Mr. Stick had recommended.

It was a re-embodiment ritual. According to a single apocryphal account, the ritual could restore a dead person's spirit to his body, but only if death was recent, body and spirit were in close proximity, and the corpse was physically reanimated when the ritual was performed. It would have been useless to June, whose body was too-long dead, but it was exactly what I needed to survive what was coming, assuming the account was more than fabrication.

The ritual itself was straightforward, requiring nothing but the reading of a chant, a wad of pine sap, and nine candles. I began my preparations with one of my mother's old cassette tapes: a copy of The Smiths' *The World Won't Listen*. I Scotch-taped over the cassette's absent punch-tab, allowing me to record my own voice over the songs. I snapped the cassette back into place, pressed Record and Play together, and read the ritual's chant aloud for ten minutes. Then I walked around the house and gathered nine candles.

I found three tea candles, two tapers in candlesticks, a Virgin Mary jar candle, and three scented votives: gingerbread, beach breeze, and evergreen. In lieu of pine sap, I carved a chunk of wax off the evergreen candle and crammed it into my pocket.

As luck would have it, I already possessed a phial of coma milk, an ink-black potion I'd acquired with surprising ease the previous winter from a classified ad in a century-old newspaper. I took everything to the bathroom, along with the toaster from my kitchen, and then I roamed around the house again, using my rising optimism like a divining rod until I located the centipede queen nestled in the pantry. She stood and uncoiled as her children swarmed toward me.

"I need your help," I said. "Can you understand my words? Wave your left antenna for yes and your right antenna for no."

She waved both antennae. I trusted she could hear me.

"June's in trouble. She's in the house under the basement and I need to get her out. Mr. Gormly said I should bring you along. Your energy might provide a measure of defense."

Left antenna: yes.

"You'll help me find June?"

Every left antenna in the room waved yes.

"Follow me," I said, heading back toward the bathroom with the queen and her brood behind me like a flashflood of centipedes.

I asked them to wait in my bedroom, just outside the bathroom door, while I finished my arrangements.

First I plugged an electric timer into the wall's rusty outlet. The timer was a plastic dial with its own receptacles, into which I plugged the cassette recorder and an extension cord. Next I took a length of twine and tied one end around the heating elements in the toaster. I hung the toaster over the bathtub by tying the free end of the twine to the ceiling light. Then I duct-taped the toaster's carriage level into the "on" position and connected the toaster to the extension cord.

I placed *The Book of Elements*, opened to a random page, on a stool beside the tub. After placing the phial of coma milk on top of the book, I arranged the candles in three-point clusters at the head, foot, and outer side of the tub, so the three triangular arrays formed a larger triangle.

While my clawfoot tub filled with cold water, I went to the kitchen and took the ice trays out of the freezer, and then I returned to the bathroom and twisted the trays over the tub. Thirty-two cubes bobbed pitifully on the surface.

"I've got it," I said to the centipede queen, who coiled with her brood and watched me, from the hallway, with patient curiosity.

I lugged a pair of utility buckets up to the roof and packed them full of snow. After three trips up and down, I'd turned the bathwater into slush, and then I stood back for a wider view of the bathroom and ran through a final, mental checklist of everything I'd prepared.

I turned to the queen in the bedroom and said, "Here's the

plan. I'm going to drink the coma milk, drown myself in the ice bath, and exit my body as a ghost. Once I'm disembodied, we'll go together into the basement. Mr. Gormly's safe is an entrance to the underhouse. I've already unlocked it, but you'll need to open the safe's door to let us in. Once we're through, we'll find June and bring her back here. Then I'll resurrect myself. When the electric timer switches on, the cassette player will recite a chant I recorded, the toaster will burn the twine and drop itself into the bath, and I'll be jolted back to life safe and sound, good as new."

It had felt somewhat simpler when I'd planned it all out.

"Did you understand that?" I asked the queen.

She indicated *yes*.

I lit the nine candles around the tub and knelt in front of the timer. An hour seemed too long, and thirty minutes seemed too short, so I set the timer to forty-five minutes and depressed the cassette recorder's play button.

I finished undressing and stood naked in the cold bathroom, feeling a warm rush of vigor and adrenaline and fear. I couldn't risk the panic, or the lure of hesitation, of dwelling on the fact that I would imminently die. I closed my eyes tight and visualized June, a woman I had never seen but knew beyond doubt. I saw her as completely as a clear ray of light: invisible, illuminating everything it touched.

I tucked the piece of evergreen wax into my cheek and forced myself to step into the slush-filled tub. Cold clamped my legs, and even with the slush barely to my knees, the shock rose up and made my abdomen contract. I squatted down and scooched myself underwater, shuddering into a groan with only my head above the surface.

I took the phial off the book, removed the stopper, and

drank the coma milk. It felt like gulping Novocain. My tongue lolled, my throat relaxed, and I didn't swallow so much as feel the black fluid flowing into my stomach, where it seeped into my bloodstream with preternatural speed. My thigh muscles sagged. I dropped the phial and my arms slumped into the slush. My vital organs and my thoughts remained unaffected; I breathed and stayed lucid as I slouched toward paralysis.

My head began to sink. I had intended that, of course, having drunk the coma milk to overcome my survival instincts once I started drowning, and yet I regretted it and panicked when my face slipped under.

Slush filled my mouth because I couldn't close my jaw. I couldn't close my eyes, either, and through my partially opened lids I saw the chilled, blurry halo of the ceiling light above me. I tried sitting up but none of my limbs responded. When the slush reached my throat, I gasped involuntarily and everything in my chest spasmed and constricted. My sinuses filled. Bubbles burbled up and out of my body.

Pressure built inside me from the weight of flooded lungs and darkness fluttered inward from the edges of my vision, closing off the dull gray light above the tub. My oxygen was gone, my sense of time unraveled, and my thoughts started losing their coherence and precision. Every part of me was screaming no no no no no.

"Live," I thought. "Die."

I was thick, cold meat. I was heavy and repulsive.

"Die," I thought. "Live."

I was fading. I was darkness at the bottom of the tub.

Then my thoughts became a deep and tranquilizing hum and everything was quieter. Everything was soft. The slush felt as comforting as warm, smooth jelly and the light around my face turned aqueous and pink. The pain was gone. My body felt beautifully cocooned.

I heard a sort of voice that was muffled and familiar, speaking in a language more musical than verbal. It was asking me a question of astonishing importance—a question I had heard before and afterward forgotten.

I answered it. I didn't speak the words but knew the meaning.

There was lightness, then. I moved my arm and felt that it was rising, followed by my other arm and finally my head. My face broke the surface of the water in the tub and I was up, I was standing and alive again.

Alive!

I saw my own face, lard-thick, underwater.

No sight of myself in a photo, no contemplative gaze in a mirror, no encounter with Other William compared to the self-estrangement of standing over my own dead flesh. My disembodied feet were standing in my corpse's pelvis, and I couldn't see them until I stepped out of the bath and stood, without dripping, on the bathroom floor.

My ghostly form was like an especially vivid mental projection. I saw my ethereal arms, navel, penis, and knees not with vision but with consciousness. They were just as I remembered from existing in my body but with all the limitations memory entails. When I focused on my hand, the knuckles and fingers looked familiar, but the lines of my palm, of which I had no precise recollection, were fluidly elusive.

I felt no cold or warmth. I felt neither the linoleum underfoot nor the vertical pressure of my gravitational weight. I touched my face and felt the contact on both my cheek and hand, and yet it was closer to a memory of a touch than literal touch. Although I had stood in the slush, and briefly in my own lifeless body, I wasn't able to move or pass through solid objects. When I leaned against the edge of the tub, I experienced only my inability to press through the metal. I swatted at the toaster dangling from the ceiling and my hand simply stopped. The toaster on the twine didn't even quiver.

I could see and hear everything in the bathroom—the wavering candles, the tiny bubbles escaping from my body's mouth and nostrils, and the atonal keening of the radiator's pipes—but my sensory perception was as limited as June's. Sight and sound dimmed outside of a minor sphere. I couldn't hear the radiators elsewhere in the house, and even my adjoining bedroom blurred and darkened a few yards beyond the door.

The centipede queen and her brood stood outside the bathroom.

"I'm here," I said and waved my arms.

They either saw and heard me physically or sensed me immaterially, because they rippled in response, shuffling in place with hundreds of legs, and affirmatively waggled their antennae in reply.

"My God," I said. "It's real. I'm actually a ghost."

Astonishment grew in place of shock. I felt euphoria without the usual lightness of breath and fear without intestinal distress. It was all so bodilessly dreamlike and pure. Unaware that I had leaned my legs against the tub, I lost balance and tumbled in backward, folding at the waist, and wound up sitting sideways with my head, upper chest, and lower legs out of the slush.

The fluid had offered some resistance but I had in fact sunk. I hadn't sunk, however, back inside my corpse. I sat atop my legs as I'd have sat on any object. Apparently once I'd left the bath, the severance had been final. I was locked out of my body and only the ritual I'd prepared—assuming it was genuine—would let me back in.

In less than forty minutes, the electric timer would start the ritual with or without me, and so I climbed back out of the tub, hurried from the room, and made my way toward the underhouse.

The centipedes followed me through the house and into the basement, the little ones tumbling down the stairs like Slinkies and the queen moving gracefully with balanced undulations.

Although my visual field was limited, I saw my way clearly in the unlit basement. Apparently vision in the dark was a benefit of ghosthood, but the more important benefit, ready to be tested, would be entering the underhouse and possibly surviving.

I stood in front of the iron safe and hoped Mr. Gormly hadn't relocked it. I touched the queen's antennae and concentrated hard, speaking aloud but trying to express myself by feel.

"I need you to open the safe," I said. "When you do, the underhouse's influence will billow up around us. Your energy ought to shield us, but once we're all inside, you'll need to close the safe behind us so the upper house's atmosphere isn't fully poisoned."

I let go of her antennae.

"Does that make sense?"

She indicated *yes*.

I moved aside as the queen approached the safe and cocked her head sideways like a smart, curious dog. After a long hesitation, she hooked a foreleg around the safe's handle, cranked it down, and opened the door.

The underhouse's influence erupted from a cavity in the bottom of the safe and flowed around the queen like blown, black smoke. Only it wasn't truly smoke but vacancy and loss, seeming to negate whatever it consumed. It didn't just conceal

Mr. Gormly's barricade but almost seemed to blot it from my memory, leaving behind an anxious, hopeless sense of its erasure. If I hadn't hunkered down with the queen and all her children, I might have lost sight of them and thought I was alone.

The atmosphere's effects were less debilitating than when I'd physically experienced them, but even in the aura of the centipedes' benevolence, my plan to find June seemed fatally absurd and I stepped in front of the queen, toward the safe, with mounting dread. The hole that led to the underhouse was emptier than black, as if a hole-shaped thing had vanished from existence. I discerned no ladder, let alone what lay below, and since I didn't have lungs with which to draw a steadying breath, I pretended to inhale, accepted my fear, and climbed inside.

14. INTO OBLIVION

When I was young, I would sometimes imagine falling into a bottomless well. I'd never imagined doing so intentionally, however, and as soon as I entered the safe and left the centipedes behind, the nothingness engulfed me and I felt as if I'd been falling all my life—that dropping into the dark was my eternal, natural state and anything else I'd felt or known hadn't truly happened.

When I landed in the underhouse, silently and with no sensation of impact, the atmosphere was so impenetrable, I couldn't at first perceive any of my surroundings and wasn't even convinced I'd stopped falling.

My vision gradually strengthened. The light was like moonlight diffused through a cloud, showing more with shadow than with direct illumination. I imagined seeing my hand until it came into view. I thought of my feet and there they were, just as they had been before I'd climbed into the safe.

Suddenly the centipedes were raining down around me. Once the little ones had landed, the queen followed suit. I stepped aside, admiring her elegant flow of legs as she cascaded down and cheered me with her liveliness and poise.

"Did you shut the safe behind you?"

She indicated yes.

Their influence slightly mollified the pestilential climate and I discovered we were on the upper landing of the underhouse's stairway. Apparently we'd entered through an underground roof. As Mr. Stick had told me, the landing was structurally identical to my own house's upstairs landing, but the ceiling bowed inward, the floorboards were warped, and the brick walls had bled mud that had coagulated into dark, sludgy scabs. Everything around us seemed in danger of collapse.

I felt that I belonged there and didn't know why. The house overhead—my snug, familiar home—seemed unreasonably distant and possibly unreal. I missed it as I often missed people I had known but couldn't quite remember why I'd ever known them.

I walked downstairs with the centipedes behind me, thankful of my weightlessness on the dilapidated steps but worried that the hundred-pound queen would break through. We reached the underhouse's third floor, which again resembled that of my ordinary house except for its state of neglect and subterranean wrongness.

A nearby window had been bricked up tight. Another window had imploded and a landslide of earth had poured through the sash. Nightcrawlers glistened in the mud and broken glass.

I expected to find June deeper in the underhouse but felt compelled to check some of the third floor's rooms, as if whatever they contained couldn't be avoided, like corners of myself that needed to be seen.

I walked down the hall to look in the oddments room. I opened the door and stepped inside, recognizing the space, the metal wall shelves, and the unlit twenty-two-watt lightbulb hanging from the ceiling.

In place of the usual curios, tools, and vintage equipment was an entirely different hodgepodge of castoff items.

Dresses, shirts, and rumpled hats. Brushes clogged with hair. Lockboxes. Jewelry. Big and little mirrors. There were keepsakes ranging from decorative figurines to trophies and certificates. Well-worn dolls and faded old toys. Photographs, framed and unframed, of people who had lived—judging by their clothing and the quality of the pictures—at various times throughout the previous century.

It was a trove of personalities, a rummage sale of lives. I knew without question that every item had once belonged to someone now dead, and I scanned the room until I recognized my mother's favorite sweater. It was caramel and cableknit, with holes in the each of the elbows, and draped across the back of the chair in which I'd seen her die.

Under the chair I saw my coffee mug—my favorite orange mug—and realized it had also once belonged to someone living.

I left the room and shut the door before I noticed anything else. The centipedes looked wary of my distress and kept their distance, walking quietly behind me, when I continued down the hall to the unfurnished room where I'd talked with Other William.

Inside I saw the wooden chair, its spindles loose and fractured, and the hospital-green plaster covering the walls. Much more of the plaster had cracked away from the underlying brick, and the baseboards were coated with its chips and moldy powder. Half the floorboards were gone and I could see the ancient joists, and the door to Other William had been boarded shut with the ripped-up flooring. Whoever had done it had used dozens of nails, some flush and many mangled, and had lodged the old hammer into the wood by its claw.

I entered the room and stared at the nailed-up boards, knowing Other William did the same beyond the door. Which of us had ultimately driven June away? Was it his fault I'd come, or had I forced him? I wished I wasn't a ghost and could grip the hammer. I wanted to pry the boards off to look at him, or bludgeon him, but he was ghostly, too, now—invisible, unkillable—and only pure oblivion would free us from each other.

I returned to the hall and strode to the stairs, passing through the centipedes as if they weren't there and almost, in my haste, moving out of the safety of their company's protection. They followed me down to the second floor, where I walked directly to my study and found the kitchen there instead.

I backed away, disoriented, double-checking my surroundings and determining that, yes, the kitchen was inexplicably where my study should have been. It didn't make sense if the layout of the house and the underhouse were identical, and I entered the kitchen with a vertiginous sense that my perception was deranged and couldn't be relied on.

The refrigerator was closed but grimly rusted, and I couldn't shake the thought that there was a child dead inside it. The linoleum floor was bubbled and loose. The ceiling was bowed and water-stained. My mortar and pestle sat on the counter, the former containing a mass of red-brown sludge that looked alarmingly fresh and wet, as if whatever it had been had only just been pulped. Over the sink, the window showed a vast night sky, rich black with glittering stars that somehow seemed dangerous, like particles of glass threatening to swarm. How any sky was visible underground defied comprehension, but before the view truly unsettled me, the ghost wife entered the kitchen in her nightgown, picked up her paring knife, and took her place in front of the sink.

She smoked her cigarette and waited, exactly as she usually

did in the normal house's kitchen, but then she looked at me directly and I took a step back.

Her eyes were clear and lancing through her cat's eye glasses. She could see me and I stopped, frozen by her stare, while the cigarette burned itself out between her fingers. The husband should have appeared by then. But I knew he wasn't coming. The wife walked toward me with the knife against her hip, expressionless and fluid in the soft-lit room. I backed away in horror when she calmly raised the blade, convinced by her intensity and menace she would cut me.

Then the wife disappeared and I was standing on a bloodstain. I recognized the stain but didn't know why. The shape of it. The feel. Even the fact of recognition felt elusively familiar until I looked around and realized I was standing in the study.

The centipedes were with me, curiously watching.

"How did we get here?" I asked the queen. "The woman. Where'd she go?"

The queen cocked her head as if she didn't understand. I noticed she was paler and her eyes looked filmy. The little ones huddled underneath her trunk.

"Are you all right?"

The queen answered yes but her antenna sagged.

The underhouse's atmosphere was stronger than it had been, and the air was full of drifting ash and smoldering flakes of paper. The study's bookshelves were empty—that was what had burned, every book in my collection—and the dark brick walls were like the innards of a chimney, blackened with a film of creosote and soot.

"This isn't right. We need to hurry. Can you sense where June's hiding?"

The queen replied *no*.

"I think I know which room she's in. I only hope the rooms stay where they belong."

I led the way into the hall and headed for the rear staircase, wary of every door and glancing backward over my shoulder, worried the knife-wielding wife would suddenly reappear. We passed my bedroom and I resisted glancing in, intuitively knowing June wasn't there and dreading what *was*. I put it from my mind and hurried downstairs, but when I reached the last step and swung around the newel post, I wasn't in the first-floor hall as I'd expected.

I was standing in the bedroom I'd passed upstairs, as if the underhouse had made the choice of forcing me to enter. Instead of a moldered or abhorrent version of my room, the space was a perfect replica with a clean-sheeted bed, orderly nightstand, and unwarped floor. The pressed-tin ceiling was just as I remembered it. From outside the window, a streetlight's glow lit the foggy glass and I wondered—with a swirl of worry and hope—if I had inadvertently transported myself out of the underhouse and safely back to my above-ground home.

The bathroom door was open. Candles flickered on the floor and the toaster dangled from the ceiling fixture. I approached the tub and saw my body in the slush—cold, well-preserved, and wonderfully familiar.

The Book of Elements was open on the stool as I had left it, and the words, like veins and capillaries just below skin, coursed with blood and slithered into new configurations. All I had to do was stare at it and wait until the language was as vivid and coherent as my thoughts.

I sensed Other William with his own *Book of Elements*. I pictured him alone. He was picturing me, too. We watched each other silently, internally, intensely, and it didn't matter which of us was thinking anymore because we both had the same objective realization.

"Of course," I thought. "It's really this simple after all."

I was weightless, effervescent—a ghost made of fizz. I'd killed myself and ventured into the underhouse for June and everything had led inevitably here. The book was offering itself. It wanted me to use it. The alternative was searching through a maze of shifting rooms while the underhouse strengthened, the centipedes weakened, and the time to resurrect myself was quickly running out. Every problem I encountered also risked June, but the book could take us back—all of us together. It was the simpler, safer way and June would understand. She would always be a ghost but at least she'd exist. She'd be loved. Even limbo was better than oblivion.

Other William's answer filled me like ink.

"You're lying to yourself because it's easy. And you know it."

I turned away from the book and concentrated hard, wishing I could grind my knuckles into my eyes and force him out of my thoughts.

"Damn it," I said. "He's right."

Once I saw it his way, I couldn't see it otherwise. The book's open pages wrinkled up and dried, its writing grayed and sagged like varicose veins, and a gas of putrefaction shimmered off its surface.

I walked out of the bathroom and my ghost felt gravely less substantial than before, as if a process of fading or diffusion was occurring. I exited the bedroom and found myself in the hallway I'd originally expected. But no other doors were visible, the stairs had disappeared, and when I turned to look behind me, the bedroom had vanished.

I stood in a corridor that extended out of sight in both

directions. Whichever way I looked, the floor canted downward, and when I chose a direction and started walking forward, the angle of decline steadily increased until eventually I felt that I was facing straight down.

The centipedes followed and we walked for several minutes. The light had dimmed. I seemed to be a mile underground. When we finally reached the end of the hallway, a radiator stood against the wall, cold and quiet, and a single slender doorway opened to the right.

Even before I reached the door, I knew I'd find the dining room and through it, farther back, the room with the indoor tree. It was the place I'd hoped to find. The underhouse had led me there.

The centipede queen stumbled against the wall. She had drooping antennae and dull, vacant eyes. Her brood had crawled up and slumped across her back, covering her trunk and delicately quaking. The queen lowered her head as if to press forward through a strong, toxic wind she couldn't overcome.

"It's OK," I said. "Go. You can't endure this anymore."

She looked too stupefied to comprehend my words. I touched my fingers to the tips of her antennae, channeling my meaning as directly as I could.

"Go back to the regular house. If the safe is locked, bang on the door till Mr. Gormly lets you out."

She wobbled side-to-side in torpid hesitation.

"Take care of your children now," I said. "I'm sorry I involved them. This is a bad place, worse than I expected. Even for you."

She seemed to sigh in relief, maternally absolved of leaving me alone. I rubbed the sides of her head and said, "I couldn't have gotten this far without you. I'll find June and get her out somehow. Go on. I'll see you soon. If I don't, though, thank you."

She leaned against me as she turned, curving through me with a body-long, affectionate caress and filling me with a final charge of centipedal strength. I watched her walk away until she darkened out of sight. I knew the shifting house would show her how to escape because it didn't want the centipedes. It wanted me and June.

I entered the dining room to snow—not a dusting but a squall—that fell in burly flakes and covered the table, chairs, and floor.

Hip-high drifts swelled along the walls. I looked up, trying to see beyond the downy chandelier and wondering, like a child, if the snow fell from someplace infinitely far. The falling flakes followed the contour of my ghostly silhouette and turned me into a walking negative space amid the whiteout.

I followed a shallow path between the table and the wall, and it was strange to move in a blizzard, seeing the snow and hearing its hiss, without feeling chilled or leaving any prints. I wasn't exhaling vapor, and my lack of breath made the wonderland's beauty seem illusory and dead. I was imaginary, moving through imaginary weather, and I slumped and pressed my nonexistent face into the snow.

I didn't suffocate. I didn't have eyelids to close. White stayed white because the room's sourceless glow passed through my head and lit the underlying snow. I turned my thoughts to sightlessness in order not to see, like staring at a wall until the wall disappears, and what a relief it was to blank my mind in meditative blindness, forgetting where I was and what was happening around me. I wanted to stay there and rest. I wanted to be blank inside the blank, peaceful snow shushing down around me.

Miniature sparks said: *Get up. Move. June.*

I let myself see and forced myself up. The room was different then, in quality if not in true appearance, as the whiteout leant an outdoor vastness to the space. I walked until I reached another open doorway that was absolutely black: a void in perfect white.

I stepped through and into the adjoining room. The light there was feeble, the snow was almost silent, and the much finer flakes drifted up instead of down, rising from a floor where no snow had settled and materializing endlessly in gentle whirls and eddies.

It rose between the branches of the sideways tree. The tree was dead. Its limbs had sloughed their bark, exposing inner wood that looked porous and diseased. Instead of little bees bobbing around the twigs, gluey termites writhed and burrowed into the branches. Fallen leaves had rotted into a moist, brown slurry that oozed over the ground moss. The moss itself was gray.

I heard the sound of frozen wood threatening to crack. Moving deeper into the room, I saw a deer with massive antlers tangled in the tree. Its neck was unnaturally twisted, and its antlers were so enmeshed with the branches, they looked as if they'd permanently woven with the wood. The deer's hooves were off the ground and its broken hind legs hung limply from its hips. Its hide twitched and crawled. Its eyes were filmy white.

"I was wrong," the deer said. "Holding on is pointless. Life is only death waiting to become."

I recognized his voice from countless conversations.

"Dad. You're alive," I said.

"Only in your head. Same as Mom. Even your memories of us will die when you die."

"I'll be someone else's memory."

"They'll die, too."

Snow flurried up, intermittently obscuring him. His snout

and teeth were feral but uncannily familiar. I imagined how his whiskers might feel against my cheek.

"I miss you both," I said.

"Stop holding on. You're torturing yourself. Let it all go because it's all going anyway."

He tried to move his head but his antlers gripped the branches and the torsion on his skull contorted his face in pain. His tongue lolled. Saliva stretched downward from his lip, immediately freezing into a slender thread of ice.

I followed his vacant gaze toward the tree's knotty trunk, where a body crouched tightly in a shadow-gust of snow. It was her, so uniquely I could smell her in my memory. I lapsed in her direction, falling like a cold draft of air between the branches.

She was younger than I had ever known her, a naked woman barely out of adolescence. She sat on the dismal moss under the sideways trunk, hunched forward in a ball with her head down and her arms wrapped tight around her shins. Her hair concealed her face and draped her gangly legs. She was pigeon-toed. Her spine made a ridge along her back and she had starburst freckles on her shoulders and her arms.

I went to her side and huddled next to her, hesitant to talk because I feared she wouldn't answer. She didn't seem to notice me. She didn't seem to breathe. I reached toward her hair and some of it rose to meet my fingers, just as ordinary hair levitates with static, but my hand passed through her. She was a ghost after all, a memory of life as insubstantial as a sentiment I couldn't quite name.

I kept my hand inside her middle, underneath her heart. I'd belonged there once and wanted to again. The more I wished, the more I felt the hopelessness of wishing. I'd put my faith in ghosts because I needed something permanent, but even ghosts were temporary. Nothing really stayed.

The empty space between us grew to feet, and then to yards, till even the memory of touching her drifted out of reach. Snow floated through me. I was thinner than the air. I chose not to look through the branches for the deer. I chose not to think about the reason I had come. I chose not to move. I chose not to feel.

When there was nothing but my choice, I chose not to choose.

15. AFTERDEATH

But somehow, essentially, I still felt alive.

Was it possible to be without a body or a thought? What vitality existed under commonplace perception that was neither hope nor memory but something in between?

I felt being felt.

It was akin to being watched, or thought about, or known. I couldn't sense a thing but someone sensed me and I was rippling like an inkling in another person's dream. I felt my ghostly hand holding someone else's hand. I saw the tree again and heard the snow's whispery ascent, and when I looked to where my mother had been, June was at my side.

She had shoulder-length hair of indescribable color. Her face was round and plain—pretty in a way that wasn't instantly apparent, like a pigeon with an extra wing folded in concealment. She was short and almost plump, sitting naked with her feet tucked beneath her bottom. She looked as if she'd woken from a strange, sad nap and found her best friend sitting in the room. I imagined my expression looked the same way.

"AM I DREAMING YOU?" she asked.

"Whatever you're doing, keep it up."

"YOU CAME FOR ME."

"I did."

"ARE YOU REAL? YOU DON'T SEEM REAL."

"I made myself a ghost."

She paled, or rather lost the saturation in her face.

"It's reversible," I said as bravely as I could. "I'm sorry I hid the book from you. June, I'm so sorry. I've been dead for half an hour and it's terrible. I hate it. Wherever you're supposed to be, it isn't here in limbo. You deserve something better than a half-life here."

"YOU KILLED YOURSELF FOR ME?"

"I couldn't let you vanish."

The snow was like static on an old TV. Everything around us was an indistinct signal but my words hung between us, startling and clear.

"YOU'RE AN IDIOT," she said. "I MEAN IT'S BALLSY AND AMAZING THAT MADE YOURSELF A GHOST EXCEPT IT'S ABSOLUTELY BONKERS. WHAT IF YOU'RE STUCK THIS WAY, TOO? I'LL SPEND THE REST OF MY EXISTENCE FEELING GUILTY THAT YOU'RE DEAD. YOU'LL REGRET IT. YOU'LL RESENT ME."

"I have a plan."

"I HOPE SO."

"Mr. Stick, the centipedes, and Mr. Gormly helped. But first we need to go before the underhouse traps us."

"THE UNDERHOUSE?"

"This place. The house we're in is real."

"I KNOW IT'S REAL," she said. "I'VE BEEN IN EVERY ROOM. I JUST NEVER KNEW IT HAD A BORING, LITERAL NAME. NOW I ALMOST FEEL EMBARRASSED THAT I WALLOWED HERE SO SERIOUSLY."

I stood amid the branches and looked around the room, afraid I'd see the deer corpse staring through the snow and wondering if June and I could really get away. The tree was either closing in or growing more complex, and we seemed increasingly surrounded by the tangle.

June stood next to me and said, "LET'S CALL IT SOMETHING ELSE. LIKE THE EXISTENTIAL DREAD HOUSE."

"I don't see the door."

"OR THE UUUBER SPOOKY SAD HOUSE. OR THE UNFUNHOUSE."

"This is serious," I said. "We need to get out of here before it starts affecting us again."

"I *AM* GETTING US OUT."

I clutched my head in consternation but my fingers passed through.

"I don't understand. Humor gets us out?"

"DIDN'T YOU KNOW?" June said. "CORNY JOKES CAN CURE DESPAIR AND SUICIDE AND EVERYTHING. WE SHOULD HAVE SUMMONED MAD LIBS INSTEAD OF THE BOOK OF ELEMENTS."

"Does sarcasm work?"

"ANYTHING CAN WORK."

"Please," I said. "I'm tired and scared and want to get us home. Tell me what to do."

"IT ISN'T ONE THING LIKE HAPPINESS OR HOPE. WHENEVER I'VE SUNK HERE BEFORE, IT WAS YOU I FOLLOWED OUT. IT COULD HAVE BEEN ANYBODY, THOUGH. ANY CONNECTION. ANY CHANCE. ALL WE'RE TRYING TO DO IS SPIRAL OUT INSTEAD OF IN."

I turned to her directly and our faces came close, enough so that the rising snow didn't float between us but surrounded us together like a flowing white halo.

"LOOK AT ME," she said. "TELL ME WHAT YOU SEE."

"I see your wide-set eyes. They're big the way you said. I see the birthmark on your back. I can see it right through you, like a curved tongue of fire in the middle of your body."

"WHAT ELSE?"

"You said you had a crooked tooth. I know it's there. I like it."

"GOOD," she said. "MORE."

"You're naked."

"SO ARE YOU."

"We're comfortable this way. We see each other now, the way we really are. It doesn't matter that you were the only ghost living in the house. You're the one I met and got to know and fell in love with."

She touched me and I recognized a sweet kind of sadness, like a two-drink buzz, that always disappeared the moment I enjoyed it.

"I DIDN'T FALL FOR YOU," she said. "I'M SORRY IF THAT HURTS. I JUST NEVER DROPPED MY GUARD BECAUSE I DIDN'T WANT TO STAY. I CARE ABOUT YOU, THOUGH. I WISH WE'D MET BEFORE I DIED. THAT'S PROBABLY NOT A THING YOU REALLY WANT TO HEAR."

"It's OK. I mean it isn't, but I'm used to it," I said. "I love my parents, too. They haven't loved me back in years. And maybe it's me, or maybe it's death, but either way, I have to live with it."

"WILLIAM..."

"Don't be sorry. Even when I had bugs in my hair, and choked on fire, and couldn't stop crying—even when I hated feeling so alone—I didn't want to quit. Other William didn't, either. This place tried convincing me I didn't want to live, but now I want my body back. However much it hurts, I want to be alive."

"YOU'RE GOOD AT THIS," she said.

"What?"

"LOOK AROUND."

The room and tree vanished in an upwind of snow that blinded me with white as absolute as dark. Out of the blankness, I began perceiving large, amorphous shapes that clarified themselves into objects I knew. Rectangles met and formed into walls. A cloud-blurred sun became a round electric light. Mounds of snow resolved into a radiator and toilet, and a deep wintry pool was actually a tub.

I saw the candles still flickering on the chipped tile floor. The book was open on the stool, the toaster dangled from the ceiling, and my corpse had the rubbery look of mozzarella cheese.

"I KNOW THIS," June said, sounding comforted and spacey.

"It's home," I said. "We made it out. We're standing in the bathroom."

"NO, I MEAN THE SONG. MY PARENTS USED TO PLAY THIS."

I'd been focused on the sights and hadn't noticed there was music. I turned to the cassette player lying on the floor.

"Oh, God," I said. "I never rewound the tape with my recording. It was supposed to play a chant that brings me back to life."

"SO THIS *ISN'T* A SPECTACULARLY WEIRD ROMANTIC GESTURE."

The toaster, faintly smoking, had started to burn the twine

from which it hung above the tub.

"It's a re-embodiment ritual," I said. "The candles, the recorded chant, and finally—"

The toaster fell. It banged off my corpse's elevated knees, tumbled into the slush, and electrified the bath. The circuit breaker tripped, stopping the music and failing to resuscitate my body, and the bathroom dimmed to a candlelit glow.

I felt legitimately ill, physically and gravely, and swayed as if I might lose balance and collapse. My thoughts hyperventilated. Everything revolved. I huddled on the floor and June crouched beside me, moving her hand along my spine as if the two of us were solid.

"YOU REALLY THOUGHT A TOASTER MIGHT ZAP YOU BACK TO LIFE?"

Her tone was one of loving and amused incredulity.

"The candles and the chant were more important than the toaster. Plus there's evergreen wax tucked inside my cheek. But now it's hopeless. I'll be stuck this way, same as you've been stuck."

"DUMMY, USE THE BOOK."

"Don't offer that," I said. "I've been tempted twice already. Now I'm terrified and desperate. I don't think I'm that selfless."

"I'M NOT THAT SELFLESS, EITHER. WE'LL USE THE BOOK TOGETHER."

"We can't," I said.

"WHY NOT?"

She stood in front of the book. I rose and stood beside her and the book reawakened, circulating blood through its slithering veins of writing while the pages blushed and glowed like invigorated skin. The thickest of the veins twisted into symbols that were filigreed with finer, more elaborate, odder capillaries. I felt as if the book was reading me and June, as prone to ask a question as it was to give an answer.

"What do we ask for?" I said.

"TO BE WHERE WE BELONG."

I leaned toward her on my left, she leaned toward me on her right, and then we shared the same space, half paired and half apart. We stood in front of the stool, examining the book. Two of the primary symbols on the pages wove together. Capillaries touched. Thicker veins fused until the blood coursed between them in a vitalizing flow.

"I'm starting to understand it."

"SO AM I," June said.

"I'm not ready for this yet. It's happening too fast."

We pressed together until our ghosts were fully intermingled. I was taller but I effortlessly shrank to fit her form, and she expanded into mine and we were perfectly proportioned. My head was in her head. Her chest was in my chest. Our mouths, fingers, hips, and legs were all a single form, and even our thoughts and feelings seemed to coalesce.

We had memories of bodily life, of whose I couldn't say.

Bones under muscle under fat under skin.

Blood and oxygen swishing through our ventricles and ears, rhythmic, reassuring, susurrus and smooth.

A mother's hands—hers or mine?—cradling our cheeks.

The distant smell of sunlight sparkling off pools.

Ice cream, or Irish cream, or something she had tongued, or something I remembered from the flavor of a kiss.

Softness in and out, blooming and surrounding us.

Discomfort, too, and aches: a stomach cramp, a throbbing knee.

Sadness in the shared consolation of our closeness.

We were us. We were real and we would never not have been.

The Book of Elements engorged. Its surface veins receded and the pages cleared and smoothed. It looked like half a bubble full of pink fluid with the candlelight fluttering and pulsing through its core.

We pressed our unified hands through the bubble's soft skin. Instantly my hands disengaged from June's as if my fingers and my palms were tangible again. Soon our whole arms extended into the fluid and I realized we were reaching into two different places. I wondered if my mother's mind had similarly split, half going one way, the other half another.

I could no longer feel what June was feeling with her hands. Whatever it was delighted her and mollified her fear, and she began to fizz away from me in essence and awareness.

"June," I said.

"WILLIAM."

Our names meant goodbye.

We knew each other wordlessly for one last second. Then our heads and all the rest of us were swallowed by the book.

I was suddenly alone and sinking into darkness like a dense slab of meat falling in a lake. The candlelight was gone. Everything was gone. I was me—only me, without a single trace of June—and I had never felt as solid or as infinitely lonely.

The falling stopped. I settled into deep, numb paralysis. The book had freed June and made me physical again, only something wasn't right.

I'd woken in my corpse.

I was conscious in my body but my body wasn't alive, and all I could do was lie there and languish in awareness. Without the toaster's voltage and the prerecorded chant, I was trapped inside my own dead matter in the tub, and as my helplessness and hopelessness erupted into fear, I screamed without sound. I thrashed without moving.

There was nothing I could do but feel the horror of confinement. Unable to die or sleep, hours would be days. My waterlogged corpse would languish in the tub, worthless and neglected in a house no one visited. How long before it putrefied, lost its human shape, and was a dense, jellied meatloaf stuffed with worms and bones? Would my self remain trapped even after that? Already I could feel my sanity unraveling.

Everything exploded and my vision flared white.

My muscles seized, my joints flexed. I banged the back of my head against the bottom of the tub and then my face burst up, out of the slush and into the air. I flailed my arms and legs, flopped onto the floor, and disgorged cold water from my stomach and my lungs.

The evergreen wax tumbled from my cheek. I coughed and gasped, astonished by the gorgeous rush of air and by the tingling, needling pain of oxygen and life. Breath after breath—the more I breathed, the more I ached. I was stunned and overwhelmed and gravely, deathly cold but there was candlelight and texture and solidity and weight. I smelled burnt twine. I felt my own pulse.

I saw the toaster in the bathtub. It didn't make sense until I noticed the extension cord, no longer plugged into the bathroom's blown receptacle but trailing out the door and into an outlet in the bedroom. Someone had repowered both the toaster and the cassette recorder, played the ritual chant, and shocked me back to life.

Now the second circuit had blown and only candlelight remained.

On the stool beside the tub, the swollen book was changing. The inner fluid thickened to paste, the amniotic pink turned cauliflower white, and the surface bulged irregularly and mushroomed like a tumor. It stiffened and condensed. I thought it might burst. Instead it gently scattered into a powdery cloud of spores that whirled around the room, thinned, and disappeared. The book's bony cover brittled and contracted, curling up and flaking into pale, fluttery ashes. I felt as if I'd watched the fireless cremation of a thing I'd grown from nothing or a thing I'd once been.

The centipede queen stood in the bedroom with her brood. We shared a long, silent stare of heart-deep relief while her many-legged shadow wavered in the candlelight.

"We dihh..."

I hunched and hacked.

"We did it. June escaped."

Then I stared at the extension cord trailing out of the bathroom.

"You rewound the tape and plugged the toaster back in. I was dead. You saved my life."

The queen's antenna wagged *no*.

I thought about that with stupefied surprise.

"*Gormly*. Did you see him?"

Again, she wagged *no*.

I convulsed so violently I couldn't reach a towel, so instead of covering up I huddled on the floor, bottomlessly cold, and hugged myself for warmth. The queen entered the bathroom and coiled around my body, squeezing me securely while her children scurried up and coated me like fur. They offered no heat but held my own within me, and my shivering subsided from the inside out.

Hour after hour, I swaddled myself in blankets next to my bedroom's radiator, absorbing its heat and zoning to its lachrymose sounds. I played my radio and dozed. I cried without knowing precisely what I cried for and mumbled to myself without remembering what I said.

Soggy from my hour as a saturated corpse, I urinated often. My inner heat finally stabilized with a stack of pancakes, a pint of orange juice, and a full pot of coffee, but my joints and muscles ached and every inch of my skin was freezer-burn raw. Sitting hurt. My breaths were viscous, and every ten or twenty minutes, between my common coughs, I exhaled a plume of oily gray vapor from my lungs.

My body slowly fortified with nutrients and warmth, my thoughts settled gently like flour through a sifter, and the house felt balmy and benevolently calm. Still the underhouse's atmosphere lingered in my spirit, and I felt as if a part of me had failed to resurrect.

I slept sporadically for varying lengths of time, and since I didn't pay attention to my bedroom clock, I rarely knew if I was waking from a concentrated nap or an elongated sleep. One morning I woke at daybreak. I rolled out of bed, pleasantly bewildered by a dream I couldn't recall. I made it all the way down to the kitchen, where I brewed coffee and pestled a cinnamon banana with no conscious thought of death or restoration. My brain and body moved as they had always moved before.

I anticipated an active day of reading in my study. In the depths of my assumptions, I believed she'd be with me, and I proceeded through my breakfast in habitual, groggy comfort.

Then I opened up fridge, saw the empty shelf where I had hidden *The Book of Elements*, and suddenly remembered what had happened.

She was gone.

My hoped-for day flashed and disappeared, leaving in my head a bobbing, burning afterglow. I stood on wobbly legs, hearing the coffee maker burble, and realized I'd become the kitchen's ghostly couple, moving through the memory of some lost morning. I envied them. They didn't know the difference anymore.

The day was spring-like and blustery with low-slung clouds. I tore the plastic off my study's broken sash, placed a bowl of coffee beans on the windowsill, and sat a long time looking at the sky and hoping the three-winged pigeon had left some offspring behind. When no birds of any kind visited the sill, I took a seat in my upholstered chair and tried to read a book I'd partially broiled with the fire spell.

I divided an hour between halfhearted reading and pondering the floor's mysterious moving stain. I thought of being a ghost, when my perception had been bound within a small, private sphere, and wondered if my ordinary life was any different.

A vertical bar of dusky light hovered in the doorway. I watched it for a while before believing it was real, and then I crossed the room, exited the study, and turned back around to view it from the hall. It was the gap beside the door to Mr. Stick's garden. I opened the door and stepped into twilight, following the cobbled footpath and noticing the season there had changed into fall.

Green ferns had yellowed, flower heads sagged from desiccated stems, and the trees' leaves had crisped and curled like archival paper. The atmosphere was lively as the leaves fell and drifted, twirling around my legs and crunching underfoot.

They were Polaroids again but too blanched for me to recognize any of the pictures.

The sky was luscious purple, flecked with silver stars that roamed and reconfigured, and the dirt beside the path teemed with vigorous worms. I smelled wood smoke, pumpkin guts, and sun-thawed frost on the verge of refreezing.

In the center of the garden was a ring of stacked books—a fire pit with flames rising from the middle. The books were unharmed. I couldn't tell what was burning.

Mr. Stick was sitting on the far side of the ring. I sat on the ground and faced him with the firelight between us.

"Thanks for helping me and June. It worked," I said. "She's gone."

His shape said, *I know. I'm sorry for your loss. I dreamed this for you—the fire and the leaf-fall.*

I looked around and sighed.

I could change it to a winterscape or anything you like.

"No," I said. "It's good to see the pictures burn."

We watched the leaves fall, blaze and wither in the fire, and emerge as coiling smoke I could almost understand.

"This is now," the smoke said, or maybe, "This is coming."

The sky and trees dimmed not visually but mentally, darkened by my growing concentration on the flames. What if everything was firelight, flaring and extinguishing?

"Now that I've been dead and everybody's gone, I don't know what to do."

"Find another way to live," he said.

The scream began at midnight. I thought it must be coming from my house's melted pipes until I followed the sound downstairs to the curiosities closet, opened the door, and saw the vibrating Mason jar containing the Hungarian curler.

It was the insect I'd saved after Mr. Gormly's booby trap. The hair cocoon was hovering and bristling in its jar, looking volatile and dangerous and powerfully electric. I took the jar out of the closet, carried it into the adjoining sitting room, and unscrewed the lid without considering the risk. Bright green sparks burned the webbing of my thumb. I dropped the jar, which shattered on the coffee table's edge, and covered my ears against the uncontained, excruciating sound.

When I couldn't find the hair cocoon lying in the glass, I backed out of the room to get a wider view. The curler's piercing scream broke the ceiling fixture's lightbulb and there in the dark, at the precise height from which I'd dropped the jar, the hovering cocoon glowed phosphorescent green. It looked like a caterpillar held aloft by fireflies, as beautiful to see as it was terrible to hear.

Painstruck and wonderstruck, I retreated to the downstairs bathroom and crammed cotton balls into my bleeding ears. The cotton wasn't enough, so I ran upstairs and found a pair of safety muffs I remembered seeing in the oddments room. The muffs made the pupa's scream slightly more endurable, and for the rest of the night and the following morning, I visited the room every thirty minutes to worry, wince, and marvel at the sudden metamorphosis.

Fine electric tendrils, two feet long, emanated gently from the airborne cocoon. What imago would emerge to justify its agony? I pitied it and partially regretted having spared it, but since I couldn't bring myself to mercifully destroy it now, I needed to at least bear witness to its throes.

That afternoon, I wrote a note to Mr. Gormly on my thickest stationery, working through several drafts until the brevity and tone were right.

> *Dear Mr. Gormly,*
>
> *Thank you for reviving my body with the toaster. For that, for aiding my rescue of June, and for your vigilance over the underhouse, I am perpetually in your debt.*
>
> *You're never to pay rent again. If there is anything you need or want—a full suite of amenities, for instance, or a toilet—do not hesitate to ask.*
>
> *Finally, one of your Hungarian curlers will soon emerge from its cocoon. I respect your solitude and understand if you decline, but I invite you upstairs to watch the imago's revelation, which I believe is imminent.*
>
> *I hope you'll join me.*
>
> *Your Friend,*
> *William Rook*

Instead of violating his space, I slipped the envelope under the basement door and onto the stairs beyond, certain he would find it and reply with eerie speed. After refilling my coffee mug in the kitchen, I returned to my study and walked to my desk, where a mint-scented envelope was waiting under my paperweight.

Inside it was a note that read:

> *I require nothing. Stay out of the basement.*
>
> *Sincerely,*
> *Mr. Gormly*
>
> *P.S. I have changed the safe's combination.*

Late in the day, I opened the roughhewn door that smelled of winter wreaths, sat in the wooden chair, and faced Other William. He looked weary but composed, the way a flood victim looks once they're given dry clothes and understand they've lost everything they own. We were both wearing safety muffs but heard each other clearly.

"I wasn't sure you'd be here anymore."

"I wasn't, either," Other William said. "I thought we might have blended."

"I don't think we can. We have to keep talking."

"Arguing."

"Conversing."

"Like any other person."

A gentle breeze drifted back and forth through the door. I thought about the day the two of us had fought and maybe spun around, trading places in the scuffle. Which of us was really Other William anymore? In the houses and the underhouses, here and in the afterlife, our versions of existence smeared and interchanged.

"That wasn't Mom down there."

"Of course not," he said.

"But real or not, I felt her."

"She's gone either way."

"I connected either way. But that was terrible with Dad."

Other William scowled. "I *know* that wasn't him."

"But what if he was right?" I asked. "That life is only death waiting to become."

"He was a talking dead deer in an underground house. It's idiotic trusting anything he said."

"That doesn't make him wrong."

Other William shrugged with phony nonchalance that seemed to be concealing injury or worry, giving his chilliness a blush of vulnerable warmth.

"Remember how I used to scare myself praying?" I said.

"'If I die before I wake.' That's a cruel prayer for kids."

"There was that one night—I must have been in kindergarten then—I asked Mom to tell me what'll happen when I die."

"And Mom said, 'You'll change.'"

"I didn't like that. I wanted to be me this way forever."

"And she kissed my chest and said, 'That's what memories are for.'"

"I hate that answer now."

"But here I am remembering."

"It's beautiful."

"It is."

"Even if it's sad."

We closed our eyes and sat together, quiet in the dark, comforted to know we'd always have each other.

I fell asleep that night, still wearing my safety muffs because of the pupa's ceaseless screaming, and woke for some reason at 4:01 a.m. My room was darkly visible, or visibly dark, with the streetlight below illuminating the ceiling, the dresser, and my sheeted body just enough to make everything real and chimerical together.

Something in a dream had smelled like June and I considered starting my day early—banana, coffee, books—to distract myself from the fragrance. But the scent only strengthened as I grew more alert, until I wondered if I were smelling an actual vestige of the rosemary-mint perfume I'd spilled in the closet weeks earlier.

I blinked repeatedly, trying to clear a curious distortion from my vision. It looked like very fine hair, so thin it was almost translucent, falling across my face. I sat up in the bed and the distortion immediately ended, but when I turned to fluff my pillow, another person's head was where my own head had been.

I fell to the floor and landed on my hipbone and elbow. The figure in my bed didn't react or change position, and after I stood and resituated the muffs on my head, I realized I had recognized her face before I fell.

She was the wife who appeared in the kitchen and the study. Either I'd always been asleep in my room at 4:01 a.m. or she didn't appear in my bed with perfect regularity. Regardless, there she was, awake without her husband.

She lay with her back to me, facing the empty half of the bed, and I walked around the footboard to watch her more directly. She was the oldest I had seen her, roughly eighty years old, with long gray hair and a lean angularity that made her seem, despite her wrinkly skin, childlike and fragile. She was fetal in her nightgown, with one hand tucked between the pillow and her cheek, and her other hand balled just below her throat.

She was talking to herself but I couldn't read her lips. Her features were alert, and instead of staring blankly at the wall, she appeared to be addressing someone on the bed.

She was talking to her husband. I saw it in her eyes—the same keenness she evinced whenever he entered the kitchen and she met him with the knife. I couldn't see her husband lying at her side, but she spoke to where he ought to have been and paused for his replies.

I climbed back into bed and lay on the empty half, rolling onto my side to face her and experience the husband's point of view. Her moving lips were uninterpretable—I thought she might be speaking in an unfamiliar language—so I tried to read her features rather than her words. Her expression subtly changed, lightening and shading.

Was she talking to her husband or only to herself? Maybe he had died and visited her as a ghost, invisible in the house's memory of the scene. Maybe she had play-acted half a conversation, pretending he was with her after he was gone.

Either way, she looked alone. She also looked consoled. Was it possible that both were possible together?

I fell back asleep once her apparition faded, and when I woke hours later, I lay in bed a long time, following the sunlight's movement on the sheet, in an equinox state between memory and hope. I opened my hand, palm upward on the mattress, remembering and wishing for the touch of June's finger.

She had never told me her last name or much about her life, but it wouldn't be hard getting information about a young woman who'd drowned in the river last December. I'd find an article or two and read her obituary. I'd look at photos of her face, which I was already reimagining and warping in my mind, and learn whatever I could about the woman she had been. Daughter. Friend. Tenant. Coworker. Loner. Eventually I'd visit her grave and feel as strange and otherworldly as anyone who stands above a loved one's grave.

I missed her. I suspected I would miss her on and off until I died, even once I didn't feel so haunted anymore. There would eventually be hours and seasons when other spirits, marvels, mysteries, and griefs would occupy my mind. Still her ghost, having blended with my own for a while, would always be a force moving in my body.

Sunlight cut my body perfectly in two. Everything was

quiet... curiously quiet. The Hungarian curler had finally stopped screaming. I took my safety muffs off and the morning swooshed in with sparrow song, traffic on the street beneath my window, and clarity in everything from mattress creaks to blanket rustles.

I ran downstairs in my boxer shorts and undershirt, and when I reached the sitting room with the curiosities closet, I stopped abruptly at the doorway, barefoot and wary of the broken jar's glass.

The cocoon still hovered at the level of my solar plexus. Its radiating filaments had shortened and intensified, and the verdant light was so transfixing, I forced myself to look away before it burned my retinas.

After putting on a pair of sunglasses, I sat in the doorway for the rest of the morning and into the afternoon, determined to see the end of the metamorphosis. Whenever I left to fill my coffee cup or use the bathroom, the house's other rooms looked blandly un-green. Whenever I returned, the green looked greener.

Thirty-nine hours after the hovering began, the cocoon burned away in a flash of white fire. A tiny puff of smoke drifted to the ceiling. The smell of it was similar to scorched autumn leaves, followed by the spring-like ozone of rain.

I put my coffee down and stood.

The insect remained tightly coiled in the air, impossible to see as bright, voltaic threads fluttered from its form, stretching out and grazing off the furniture and walls. Tendrils reached toward me—first a few, then the rest—as if attracted to the other living body in the room. They snaked around my arms and underneath my shirt. They touched me on the neck, as electrified as kisses. Nerves throughout my body tingled in reaction and the muscle of my heart felt bioluminescent.

The imago unfolded, marvelous and moth-like, broadening its soft green radiating wings.

Something in my chest equally unfurled. The tendrils disappeared but I was inwardly aglow, and when the insect fluttered and approached me at the door, I moved to let it pass only inches from my face and took a deep breath of its invigorating wake.

I followed it down the hall and up the rear stairs, moving through the shadows of its bobbing, spherical light. It rose in perfect silence like an up-blown feather, and when it reached the access hatch that led to the roof, it landed on the handrail, awaiting my approach.

I leaned in close to view its incandescence. The moth's proboscis uncurled and zapped me on the nose. I flinched and rubbed the burn, and my electrified nostril hairs triggered a fit of sneezing. As with any good sneezes, the explosions cleared my head, and after wiping the tears out of my eyes, I reached up and opened the hatch leading to the roof.

The day had paled. The weather had grayed. A heavy cloud's underbelly sagged above the house, and when the moth beat its wings and fluttered out the door, it sizzled in the mist drifting in the air.

I climbed to the roof and smelled the damp tar and melting snow. The moth made a sound like a sun-warmed harmonica, thawing old feelings that had long lain cold, and then it flew toward the cloud until its glow became a blur and left the brownstone below for somewhere else.

I let it go.